The Virgin & The Dragon

A Life Story of the Virgin Mary

John Hibbert

authorHOUSE®

AuthorHouse™ UK Ltd.
500 Avebury Boulevard
Central Milton Keynes, MK9 2BE
www.authorhouse.co.uk
Phone: 08001974150

© 2009 John Hibbert. All rights reserved.

No part of this book may be reproduced, stored in a retrieval system, or transmitted by any means without the written permission of the author.

First published by AuthorHouse 3/27/2009

ISBN: 978-1-4389-3054-1 (sc)

Printed in the United States of America
Bloomington, Indiana

This book is printed on acid-free paper.

INTRODUCTION

When preaching many years ago in Fermoy in Southern Ireland to a congregation of Roman Catholics a very sincere gentleman sitting on the back row raised his hand to ask a question. When I signalled my consent he politely stood to his feet and thanked me for the commitment to Christ which brought me to preach in his town and expressed his appreciation for the thought-provoking content of the sermon. He then voiced his concern. One thing troubled him. With eyes full of tears and puzzlement he said, "I just do not understand why you do not love Our Lady." He was of course referring to the Virgin Mary. He set me thinking. Who was this woman who has become the very epitome of controversy between the two halves of Christendom throughout the centuries? What is the truth about her? What was she like? Do the Roman Catholics revere her beyond what is right? Does the Protestant Church withhold due respect for one the scriptures declare to be "highly favoured" and "blessed among women"? What happened to her? And where is she now?

I decided to write her story. I have only been able to do it in a novel format because there are too many areas of her life which are open to debate, but I have remained faithful to the biblical text and the more reliable of the historic references together with some church tradition. I have, of course, used my imagination and done much reading between the lines. My research has been fed by visits to Nazareth and Lake Galilee, Bethlehem and Jerusalem, and by the wonderful privilege of standing in the garden tomb where the body of Christ was laid and where Mary came to tend the body of her son. Visits to Rome and to the ancient ruins of Ephesus, including one to a stone built house on a hill outside the town where Mary is believed to have lived and died, together with the connection with the past which can be felt at the tomb of the Apostle John, completed my geographical education.

I hope that you will enjoy reading my thoughts about this most amazing woman, probably the most important woman in the history of the world. I have enjoyed walking with her through the hills of Nazareth and tasting a little of the burden of freedom which she bore for mankind. I salute and love the memory of a pure woman of unquestionable integrity and enviable character, surely an ideal model human-being for both young and old.

PROLOGUE

Two middle-aged sisters, both of them widows, were struggling to mount the rough stone steps leading to the fortress palace of Machaeus in Parea, the retreat of Herod Antipas, Tetrarch of Galilee, and the son of the notorious Herod the Great. They had endured a long and arduous journey across the perilous Judean wilderness to arrive at the crossing of the Jordan River at the point where it empties its waters into the Dead Sea, and then embarked upon the seventeen mile trek down the eastern coast of the sea, into the Gorge of Calliroe, finally crossing the fifteen metre high bridge which connected the eastern plateau to the huge rock they now climbed. Machaeus, The Black Fortress, stood ruggedly proud, a full 700 metres above Lake Asphaltitis, more generally known as the Dead Sea. It was a foreboding and desolate place. The sun was setting into a drifting mist which was clinging lazily to the surface of the sea of salt and a chill wind swirled around the rock to impede their progress. The hooded figures of the women, silhouetted against the half light, added a cold loneliness to the gloomy scene. They clung to each other as they mounted each step, stopping at regular intervals to gather their strength. They were on their way to visit a prisoner who had languished in one of the rock hewn dungeons beneath the castle for a full ten months. He was the only son of their late cousin Elizabeth and was greatly loved by them both. They were on a mission of love to encourage him in the trial of his unjust incarceration, but they were also there out of respect and love for their dead cousin who they knew would have desperately wanted them to care for her son in his hour of need.

His name was John, son of Zacharias, known throughout Judea and Galilee as John the Baptist. His powerful preaching, exhorting people to repent in advance of the advent of the Jewish Messiah, touched the lives of thousands. He was bold, outspoken, and unusual, like an old time Prophet born out of due time. The emergence of Jesus of Nazareth had marked the fulfilment of his ministry, and, believing his job was done, he deliberately began to withdraw. He did, however, remain verbally outspoken on issues which he regarded as matters of righteousness, but he appeared to take a step too far when he raised public objection to the moral behaviour of the Tetrarch. Herod Antipas was married to Phasaelis, a most desirable Arabian princess, but whilst visiting his brother Philip he fell to the sensual charms of Philip's beautiful wife Herodias and the two of them became lovers. The torrid affair ripped their existing relationships apart and both Antipas and Herodias divorced their partners and remarried each other. The union was further tarnished and complicated by reason of the fact that Herodias also happened to be the niece of her new husband, the daughter of another of Herod's brothers. John the Baptist was incensed and proceeded to fearlessly and publicly denounce the relationship as illegal, an insult to Jewish laws and standards, and an incestuous sin before a holy God. As a consequence, and largely due to the resulting hatred which was directed towards him from Herodias herself, John was arrested and imprisoned at Machaeus. It was not common for visitors to make the journey to this forbidding place, although they were occasionally permitted. It had recently been reported to Jesus and his followers that John was in a serious state of depression and was even beginning to doubt that Jesus was the Messiah. The visit of the women was if anything overdue.

Salome and Mary shivered as darkness wrapped itself around the rock like a shroud. The wind moaned its ghostly requiem across the barren terrain in sharp contrast to the sounds of merriment, music and laughter which were drifting down from the palace on the plateau above them. The magnificent edifice was three hundred and twenty five feet long and one hundred and ninety five feet wide, crowned with spectacular ramparts complete with huge corner towers reaching ninety feet into the air. It was Herod's birthday and he was entertaining his friends, both Jews and Romans, at a banquet in his honour. He had pampered his visitors with an afternoon of relaxation in the hot mineral springs that bubbled generously in a number of the hills local to the palace, and they were now enjoying the finest of Israel's cuisine in the spacious banqueting chamber above the dungeon caves.

A single guard, a man of enormous stature, met the sisters as they approached the man-made cave which was the prison of their loved one. He was a kindly man who guided the women carefully across the rough ground, through the iron gate which kept the entrance to the cave, and into the gloomy hole beyond. Two flaming torches crudely fastened to the walls cast an eerie moving light across the unwelcoming scene. A rat scurried for cover as they approached. John was sitting in the corner of the cave chained to a metal stake that had been hammered into the stone floor. The stench of human excrement made Mary heave. It took several seconds for recognition to focus and then John let out a cry of surprise mingled with extreme embarrassment. He tried to stand but his legs were obviously seriously weakened by his ordeal and it took several attempts before he managed to gain his feet. He was naked but for a rag loin cloth tied crudely around his waist. The chains restricted any forward movement, but Salome immediately ran within the circle of confinement and embraced him warmly. Then Mary wept quietly on his shoulder. How she loved this boy she had known since before he was born. For three months she had tended his pregnant mother, many times placing her hands on her swollen belly to feel the kick of the unborn. She loved him as a boy and followed his upbringing with prayerful interest and in recent times she could put no value on the priceless service he had performed in preparation for the ministry of her own son. She stood back and gazed into the face of her cousin Elizabeth's only son. He was just thirty two years old but had the look of a man of sixty or more. He looked nervous, perhaps a little depressed.

"How is Jesus?" he asked.

It was his first question, the matter closest to his heart. He was tormented with doubt, but even more tormented with the guilt his doubt spawned in his sensitive heart. His whole life was dedicated to serving this amazing gift from God, the Christ himself, but this hell-hole was a different world from the one he had dominated in the Judean hills and by the banks of the Jordan River. He knew what it was to be isolated. He spent much time alone in the wilderness and knew many lonely hours, but this was a different kind of isolation and one that tended to doubt. He was sure that the message he sent to Jesus asking him if he was really the Messiah, or "Look we for another?" must have reached him by now and he was afraid that his doubt had betrayed his calling. His mind was a minefield of confusion and fear of failure panicked his soul. Mary's softly spoken answer came like music to his ears.

"He is wonderful, John," she replied. She leaned forward and took his hand between her own and gazed into his troubled eyes. "He sent you a message. He said to tell you that the cripples walk, the lepers are cleansed, the deaf hear, the blind receive their sight, the Gospel is preached to the poor, and the dead are raised to life again."

The prisoner breathed a huge, long sigh of relief, and then burst into tears of joy. He became animated with excitement, shouting for the guard who had retreated a discreet distance from the group. The big man came running.

"I told you he was the Messiah! Jesus of Nazareth! Have you not heard of the miracles that he has done? This is his mother, Mary, and his aunt, Salome. Oh, I give thanks to God for his goodness!"

The guard respectfully lowered his head to the women in acknowledgement of the introduction and smiled reassuringly at his prisoner.

"His name is Julius," John said, looking intently into the face of his guard. "He has been good to me. I have told him about Jesus."

Julius smiled sadly. "It is a story of powerful love," he said, turning slowly and disappearing into the shadows.

Disregarding the abominable filth of that dreadful place the two sisters sat with John for an hour or more, their hearts overflowing with compassion. They talked of fond memories of the past, the wonder of God's provision for their present trial, and their aspirations for the future. They sang a psalm together and they prayed for God's help and blessing. How the presence of God filled that unlikely and squalid place! His peace overcame the darkness and John was lifted from despair to delight, from doubt to living faith, from defeat to exhilarating victory. It was as though his stinking dungeon suddenly became the very gate of heaven. Mary asked the guard for water and bathed John's open sores. She swilled the floor in an attempt to clean the excrement from where he lay.

Meanwhile in the banqueting hall above them the feasting and revelry continued unabated. The scene was one of debauched excess. Fat and greedy men filled their bellies with roast lamb, ox meat garnished with olives and almonds, and a variety of flying fowl from blackbirds to ravens. Mute slaves carried huge platters of dates, pistachios, and luscious grapes to the reclining aristocracy. Candelabra hung from rafters of cedar wood, and flaming torches sat in silver loops around the walls of the chamber. The wine flowed and semi-naked women moved wantonly amongst the tables, seductively inflaming the passions of the men. Herodias had planned well for this special night. Unbounded hatred burned in her heart against the son of Zacharias. She was painfully aware of the impression that the prophet's words had made upon her man. Antipas was clearly troubled by the preacher's opinions and it was affecting their relationship. She wanted the fanatic silenced. She wanted him dead. Fully cognizant of the moral weaknesses of her husband, she had devised a subtle plot to exploit them to the accomplishment of her enemy's demise. How easily Antipas had succumbed to her sexual charms when she first paraded herself before him in the house of her former husband! He was a lustful man possessing minimal control over his animal passions. She was also sensible to the salacious looks he had been directing recently towards her teenage daughter, Salome. The stage was set. All she needed to do was direct the play.

Herodias solicited the help of her beautiful daughter, persuading her to enact a dance of sexual seduction as a birthday gift to her step-father on the evening of the feast. Her proposition was that at the conclusion of the performance Salome would ask Antipas for a gift, a gift which would bring a brutal revenge upon the disgusting prophet who had dared to speak against the wife of Herod. She personally supervised and attended the preparations for the dance, skilfully ensuring that her daughter made full capital of her physical assets. The music would be simple and basic. She wanted full attention on the dancer, not the music.

She patiently waited for the right moment, when bellies were full and resistance low. At the appointed time, when her husband was suitably inebriated with rich red wine from the vineyards of Engedi and aroused by the sensual atmosphere of revelry around him, she made her move. She approached the couch where he lay in his indulgence and whispered softly in his ear.

"My darling, I have a surprise birthday gift for you – look!"
She clapped her hands twice and silence fell across hall. She clapped them again, requiring stillness. The servants stood motionless. Only the lights from flickering flames disturbed the shadows on the bare stone walls. Somewhere a bell sounded.

She appeared in slow motion from behind a heavy crimson curtain to the left of the chamber. A single drumbeat accompanied her as she floated across the floor. Every eye in the building drank in the vision of this stunning, eastern beauty. Her long, raven black hair floated like a silken veil behind her, cascading hauntingly around her slender shoulders. Her huge brown eyes flashed with youthful passion and her brow was adorned with a sparkling tiara of diamonds. She was naked but for a short purple loin cloth, skilfully fitted to rest low on her swaying hips, and a narrow band of gossamer thin, shimmering silk which was wrapped loosely around her breasts, crossed over behind her back, brought round across her belly, and fastened with a golden clasp above her navel. Her feet were bare.

Antipas was visibly excited. He reached for his flagon of wine, his hand trembling with desire. The beat of the drum slowly increased in tempo and as it did so she began to move with the beat. She positioned herself before her victim, swaying from the hips, gently, from side to side, like long grass in the meadow in the soft morning breeze. She manoeuvred seductively, first forward, and then backwards, gaining momentum with the accelerating beat of the drum, bending from the waist until her hair swept the floor in front of her. She writhed and rolled and leaped in unrestrained abandonment. Her voluptuous body became wet with perspiration, gleaming and glistening in the lamplight. Then the slower beat again. She was running her hands suggestively over the contours of her body whilst unhurriedly making her final approach to the husband of her mother. She paused and arched her back until her hair teased the ground behind her. Then she stood erect, made eye contact with her prey, held his lustful gaze, enticing him with her eyes, talking to his soul, pulling him into the whirlpool of desire. She leaned over him. He could smell her perfume mingling with the sweat of her flesh. She whispered in his ear.

"Would you like to unfasten the clasp my lord?"

Timed to perfection, the drum stopped beating. Hearts pounded as in breathless silence she thrust herself forward and with trembling fingers he unclipped the golden clasp that would reveal her nakedness. In an instant she replaced the clasp with her right hand, holding the covering silk in place. She retreated now, a childlike, coy expression on her face. When she spoke it was to spring the trap that would give her mother her desire.

"Please my lord, is there nothing that you would like to give to me?"

The poor besotted fool laughed aloud in his crazed and drunken state of unbridled longing.

"Anything, my beauty! Anything you desire, to the half of my kingdom! Ask, and it shall be yours!"

For a moment Salome hesitated. She glanced across at her mother. Did she really want this?

The look of smug satisfaction and triumph on the face of Herodias was self-explanatory. She wanted it more than anything in the world. She affirmed it with a nod of her head. Salome bowed low before her stepfather.

"I would like, Herod Antipas." She paused for effect before continuing. "I would like the head of John the Baptist brought to me now on a silver platter."

The words echoed around the hall of feasting and died in a pool of stunned silence. Antipas leaped to his feet, suddenly shocked into his senses. He made an attempt to speak but no words came out. There was a long pause before Herodias began to clap her hands, slowly at first, then as others began to follow suit, more quickly. Within seconds the whole banqueting chamber was alive with base and bloodthirsty applause. The Tetrarch knew that he was beguiled. There was no way that he could renege on his promise before all these guests. He was trapped. His accursed wife had led him like a lamb to the slaughter. He struggled to gain a posture of dignity. His visitors knew that his wife had stripped him of his power. He was humiliated. His only way to save face was to appear delighted with the macabre request.

He raised his hand for silence and signalled his consent to the palace guard. The soldier turned on his heel and walked out into the night.

The guard descended the steps with an uncertain heart. As he approached the dungeon caves he saw two women making their way down the rock steps to the plain below. They were singing softly as they went, what sounded like a rendering of the great King David's 'Shepherd Psalm'. He could just make out the words as the wind carried them back up the mountain. "Yea, though I walk through the valley of the shadow of death I will fear no evil; for Thou art with me, Thy rod and Thy staff they comfort me."

He arrived at the cave which housed the preacher-prisoner and gave instructions to Julius, the soldier still on duty. His vociferous protestations were to no avail and the reluctant guard disappeared into the darkness of the cave. Some minutes passed before the voice of God's servant was lifted in a mighty "Hallelujah". The sword fell and sent his soul to its eternal reward.

Five minutes later the occupants of the dining hall drew in their breath with incredulity as the bearded head of the one known as John the Baptist, on a platter swimming and dripping with blood, was presented to the beautiful Salome. She took it in her hands and, vainly trying to avoid the blood that was dripping onto her naked feet, crossed the room to her waiting mother. She handed over the grotesque prize, turned and left the room. She felt sick.
Herodias looked with evil satisfaction into the lifeless face of her enemy but as she did so her smile faded. She felt cheated for the expression frozen into the features of the preacher by the blade of the sword was one of unutterable peace. His lips were etched with the smile of contentment. There was no fear, no anger, no resentment.

"Do you know what he said to me before he died?" Julius posed the question to the Palace Guard, but did not wait for an answer. "He took my hand in his and said 'All is well my friend, I prepared the way for Him on earth, now I go to announce His coming to the spirits in the halls of Hades'. What did he mean sir?"
"God only knows," was the reply. "God only knows what we have done tonight."

CHAPTER ONE

Another Salome, daughter of the recently deceased Heli of Nazareth in Galilee sat contentedly in her favourite place overlooking the placid waters of the lake. The day was young but the heat was already building as the sun blazed across the shimmering expanse before her, transposing the huge body of water into a gently moving mirror. She loved to watch the sunlight dancing on the rippling surface of the lake. It reminded her of diamonds, showers of diamonds, falling like raindrops into the water from a clear blue sky. She arranged the long black tresses of her hair behind her head and wound them round her fingers in an attempt to keep them from falling back around her face. It was the face of a young woman of only twenty-two years of age, yet one full of character and maturity. High cheek bones enhanced widely set eyes of deepest brown. Her slightly curved nose and full lips, set in the dusky complexion that was typical of her people, gave her a striking, handsome kind of beauty. She was of medium height and slightly heavier than she would prefer. She had never succeeded in regaining the trim, slim figure she had enjoyed before the birth of her son, though it was not for the lack of trying.

Salome smiled gently as her three year old son James made a clumsy attempt to throw a pebble into the lake. The shingle provided an uncertain platform for one so small and the stone flew backwards and he lost his footing. Undaunted he prepared himself for another attempt but it again ended in failure and the little fellow fell sprawling amongst the pebbles. Salome watched as he slowly picked himself up and brushed the dirt from his knees, more determined than ever to succeed. His display of willpower brought tears of admiration to her eyes. Eventually, more by chance than accurate aim, a sizable pebble splashed into the water and a cry of infant triumph rang through the morning air. How like his father he was. She looked across to her beloved Zebedee who had waded waist deep into the lake. He was hauling his hand nets, heavy with fish, towards the narrow beach. The muscles rippled in his sun tanned back and the wet black locks of his hair were clinging to his strong shoulders. He was a gentle giant of a man with a will of steel. How she loved him. Today was their fourth wedding anniversary and her husband had promised that he would not take the fishing boats out today. He would just fish a little with the shore nets and leave himself free to spend the rest of the day with his wife. It was a peaceful but exhilarating scene. The gulls were noisily plucking their prey from the lake. The waters at this north-western coast of the Sea of Galilee were particularly fruitful due to the copious spring waters which spilled into the lake at the small fishing village of Bethsaida, so warming the otherwise chill water. Huge numbers of fish congregated there, popping the surface of the water until it appeared to boil and hiss, attracting predators from both land and air.

Bethsaida was a small community annexed to the larger town of Capernaum. Zebedee worked hard from his early teens to build what was now a prosperous fishing business employing several men. He was immensely proud of his lovely wife and their infant son and wished for nothing more than to care for his family on the shores of this magnificent lake. He loved the sights and sounds of Galilee, the smell of the fish in the market place and the sweet scent of the crisp morning air. He revelled in the friendly competition that existed in the fishing community, especially between himself and his friend Jonas whose young son Andrew played so well with James when the young families met together. His sense of adventure was adequately challenged by the unpredictable temperament of this tiny sea with its sudden squally storms and fits of unexpected temper. He was at home in his boat, riding the waves, taming the wild water and taking his living from its depths. It was his ambition to teach his son the skills of the trade and one day have him take over the business.

He turned at his young son's cry of victory and in seconds he was splashing his way to the water's edge and lifting his giggling child to the heavens.
"Well done my boy," he laughed. He carried James into the water and swirled him round and round, trailing his toes in the water.

Salome was grateful for her spacious home in this most picturesque and fertile region of Israel. The scenery was awesome, the rugged mountains to the east cradling the matchless waters of the lake. Her home was set in a copse of eucalyptus trees and sweet smelling acacias were in abundance. Olive orchards were plenteous, local vineyards were the source of some of the richest wines in Palestine, and the superb climate ripened fruit to perfection. The cost of living was lower than that of Judea to the south. Corn was plentiful and local industries produced pottery and glass and dyes. A major road brought caravans from the east of Jordan, across the bridge of Jacob, traversing the northern coast of the lake, skirting Capernaum and then carrying them south-westward to Nazareth before turning westward to the Mediterranean coast. She knew that she was considerably better off than many others. She did, in fact, have everything she needed. It caused her considerable anguish, and more than a little guilt, to think of the young sister she had left behind in Nazareth, living alone and with considerable hardship. She was able sometimes to send her some provisions and she had made repeated offers for her to come and live with herself and Zebedee, but her sister was an independent soul and had no intention of being prised away from her roots.

Salome blinked back tears which were a mixture of guilt and gratitude as Zebedee, soaking wet from the waist down and holding a laughing James under his right arm, proffered his left hand to haul her to her feet.
"Come my love. What would you like to do today?"
"What about the nets?" she quizzed.
"I'll get someone to attend to them. Come on, where shall we go?"

An hour later they were skimming across the lake on the prettiest boat in Galilee, its white sail fluttering in a gentle breeze. Under the steadying hand and the watchful eye of his father a small boy gripped the tiller with both hands, his face a picture of excitement and joy. Salome lay back against her husband's strong chest and purred with contentment. She was smiling inside. Pure love was coursing through her veins and her soul sang to the music of the lake. She wanted to hold the moment and live in it forever. Zebedee took the tiller and swung the boat northward and the sail tightened. Her eyes roamed the mountains of Moab in the east. Wisps of heat haze danced above the wadis between the rugged hills and played tricks with her eyes. The mountains appeared to sway in gentle intoxicating movements in concert with the rise and fall of the boat, conspiring to seduce her senses. She felt dreamy. Everything seemed surreal. The beauty of creation, the mysteries of nature, the mountains with their green slopes and rugged heights, her wonderful husband and her adorable child, everything was wonderful.

"Look mummy, a bird!" James cried and for a moment invaded her illusory world of serenity. She watched as the young pelican skimmed across the surface of the water, skidding to rest a hundred metres or so away from the boat. She watched it for a moment before sliding back into her peaceful world of dreams. It was then that she thought she saw, beyond the floating bird, in the distant hills, emerging from a space between the craggy rocks, the figure of a man. He was tall and wearing some kind of uniform, like that of a soldier. He appeared to be pushing another man in front of him, a man of smaller stature than himself. Salome watched as the smaller man was forced roughly to his knees, whereupon he clasped his hands together as though in prayer, lifting his face towards the heavens. The standing figure raised his head, and then his hands above his head. At that moment the mist cleared briefly from the scene and she saw the sun glint upon the two edged sword which the soldier held aloft. She instinctively tried to stand in the moving craft, her hands rose in silent protest, as though to protect the unknown victim, but there was nothing she could do. It all happened so quickly. The sword fell. The camera in her mind suddenly zoomed in as blood splashed against the rocks and the lifeless head rolled into a nearby hollow. The executioner bent down and callously picked it up by the hair and as he began to walk back between the rocks the face swung round, bearded and bloody, lifeless eyes protruding from their sockets. It was the face of a man in middle life. She turned away in horror, then, against her better judgement, she looked back. She still had the close-up of the man's head. She gazed at his distorted blood bespattered features. Somehow, from somewhere, she thought that she recognised him. As she searched the pallid countenance the beard began to slowly disappear and then the facial features shed the years, speeding back through youth to childhood. Unexpectedly she was then gazing into the face of an infant and she shuddered violently as recognition in slow motion invaded her mind. She screamed. It was the face of her son.

She fell forward into the belly of the boat and in an instant Zebedee was lifting her in his arms and cradling her head against his shoulder. James was crying with fear for his mother.
"Salome, what's wrong? Salome, can you hear me? What happened?" Zebedee's loving concern was etched into his troubled expression. Salome stirred from her brief moment of unconsciousness and turned her pale face again towards the east, searching the mountain range for the remnants of her vision. There was no soldier, no victim, and no decapitating sword. Just the hills and the wheeling gulls, and the sun burning off the morning mist.

She held her son James considerably longer than was usual that evening when she kissed him good night and committed him with more passion into the care of the God of Abraham, and she held her sleeping husband a little closer through the hours of darkness. She hoped and prayed that her experience on the lake was a mental deception created by the sun and the mist and the movement of the water, a mere fiction of the mind. Deep within her spirit she knew that it was not, that it was rather some unwelcome premonition of a future agony. She prayed that she would never live to bury her son.

CHAPTER TWO

The aging priest gripped the golden censor with trembling hands. It contained the holy incense compounded by the apothecary for worship in the Holy Place. It contained special perfumes, stacte, onycha, galbanum, and pure frankincense. Adrenaline surged as a cocktail of apprehension and excitement coursed through his veins. He was about to step for the first time into the sanctum of sacred worship. He was born into the Jewish Levitical line and was a priest after the order of Abia. In the midsummer of the year before the birth of our Lord the priests of Abia were summoned for service in the Temple at Jerusalem. Particular duties were assigned by lot and on this particular day the lot indicated that Zacharias was to be honoured with the once in a lifetime privilege of offering incense upon the altar in the Holy Place. He nervously navigated the steps with unwavering precision. His fellow priests had completed the preparatory rituals. The sacrifice of the burnt offering was completed and the burning coals from the altar of burnt offering were safely deposited on the altar of incense. The people had withdrawn from the court and he was a lone figure as he entered the Holy Place.

Before him was an altar of pure gold standing 90cm high and 45cm square. Curved horns augmented each corner and an ornamental moulding crowned its top. On the front and rear edges were two pairs of rings provided for the reception of the golden staves which were used for the transportation of the altar. Coals of fire were glowing blood red on its surface. To his right stood the table of showbread, and to his left was a magnificent seven-branched candlestick. The flickering light from the candles served to exaggerate the eerie silence which seemed to dominate the room. The atmosphere was of a kind which he had never encountered before. He surveyed momentarily the furniture of the Holy Place before his eyes were drawn irresistibly to the heavy curtain which was hanging on the further side, beyond the golden altar. When he was a child his father told him stories about that curtain and the room which lay beyond its folds. It was the curtain which concealed the entrance to the room known as the Holy of Holies, the most sacred and feared territory in the whole of Israel. Historically it was the place of atonement. In Solomon's Temple this most holy place housed the famous Ark of the Covenant which contained the Ten Commandments which God gave to Israel through his servant Moses. Hiding the commandments from view was the golden lid of the Ark known as "The Mercy Seat", complete with its two golden Cherubim. Once a year the High Priest of Israel ventured through the curtain and sprinkled the blood of a sacrificed lamb seven times upon that Mercy Seat as atonement for the sins of the people. Symbolically the blood came between the people and the law which they had broken and provided mercy for the guilty. Zacharias knew that the room was now empty, except for the Ebhen Shethiyah, a piece of rock with only traditional and superstitious significance. The Ark and its contents were long lost, never seen since their tragic disappearance at the time of the Temple's destruction by Nebuchadnezzar, king of Babylon, in 586 BC. The aura of intrigue and mystery associated with its memory was, however, as powerful as ever. To be so close to such forbidden territory set Zacharias' pulse racing and magnetised his gaze to the silent and dangerous veil.

He shook his head clear of distraction and forced himself to engage the task in hand. He lifted the censor and cast the incense onto the burning coals before him. He paused to wait for the smoke to begin its ascent and then lifted his eyes in thankfulness to the God of Abraham. Satisfied that his duty was completed he bowed reverently to the altar and, having indulged in one final glance at the holy curtain, proceeded to back away towards the steps that would return him to the court of the priests. It was then that he was arrested by a movement to his left, from between the altar and the candlestick. The fluttering lights from the candlestick were dancing in the smoke which was rising from the altar and for a moment he thought that his eyes were being deceived by this activity. Not so, the disturbance was from another source. Clearly visible now, as though emerging from the smoke itself, was the figure of a man, yet certainly no ordinary man. Zacharias' chest tightened with fear as the being materialised before him. His strong and handsome frame was simply garbed in shimmering white linen. His countenance was beyond the natural and the priest's legs weakened as the realisation dawned upon him that he was standing before a visitor from another world. He wanted to run. This place was too terrible, too holy, too wonderful for him. He tried to leave but his feet were as heavy as lead. He tried to articulate but his mouth was dry with fear.

Then the angel spoke, softly and reassuringly, and with the sound of his voice fear took flight and was replaced with an atmosphere of unutterable peace. Trepidation turned to worshipful awe and his desire to depart was replaced with an instinct to worship. He lowered himself to his knees, to savour and absorb the wonder of the moment.

"Don't be afraid Zacharias. I have come to inform you that your prayer is heard, and that your wife Elizabeth will bear you a son, and that you must call him John. You will have joy and gladness, and many shall rejoice at his birth, for he will be great in the sight of the Lord. He shall be filled with the Holy Ghost from his mother's womb and many of the Children of Israel shall he turn to the Lord their God. He shall go before him in the spirit and power of Elijah, to make ready a people prepared for the Lord."

In an instant Zacharias was plunged into mental and emotional turmoil. He found himself trapped between the obvious supernatural nature of these happenings, for he could not deny that here in this strange and holy place, he was standing before an angelic being, and the logical absurdity of that which he was hearing. Surely the facts were clear to everyone. There was no way that his wife could bear a child. He and Elizabeth were childhood sweethearts and were married whilst still only teenagers. They made their home in the small and uninspiring town of Bet Hakerem not far from Jerusalem and for the whole of their married life had yearned to have children. Unfortunately they were unable to reproduce. Elizabeth was barren. In the Jewish culture of the time, infertility was regarded as some kind of punishment and the reproach which they both felt as a consequence of the fruitlessness of her womb was a source of great sadness and the subject of much prayer. Hand in hand the devoted couple daily knelt in supplication to the God of Israel and pleaded for a child, but all to no avail. The years rolled by and youth gave way to middle age, and middle age to the eventide of life, but there was still no answer to their cry. Many times they talked of miracles, reminding each other that the father of the Jewish nation, Abraham, had been in similar predicament centuries before and his wife had conceived and borne him a son at ninety years of age. But they both knew that theirs had been a very special case. Abraham was the recipient of a promise from God that he would make of him a great nation and certainly no such promise had been made to them. Inevitably with the passing years their prayers became void of passion, belief faded, and resignation crept into their hearts. They gave up. They were not bitter or resentful but accepted that they must serve out the rest of their days childless.

Zacharias found it impossible to believe that his beloved Elizabeth, who was now far beyond child-bearing age even if she had been a fertile woman in the past, could now bear him a son. It was absurd, to say the least. The laws of nature forbad such a thing. Maybe he was dreaming all this. Perhaps the powerful symbol of answered prayer which was symbolised in the ascending smoke rising from the altar of incense had stirred his subconscious desire for a son and cruelly inflamed his imagination. He would not, and must not, allow himself to be tormented with such fanciful and futile ideas. When he replied to the angel it was with a heart full of doubt and natural reasoning.
"How shall I know this? For I am an old man, and my wife well stricken in years."

In consequence the tone of his visitor's voice changed from one of joyful annunciation to one of subdued indignation.
"My name is Gabriel. I stand in the presence of God. I have been sent to speak with you and to bring you this good news. Because you do not believe my words you will now be dumb until the day of their fulfilment. They will most certainly be fulfilled at the appointed time."
With these words the angel turned his back and faded away into the smoke.

The people waited nervously for the emergence of the priest. He seemed to have been in the Holy Place for an uncommonly long period. They were aware of the fearsome happenings that were possible in that sacred sanctuary where Almighty God communed with mortal man. The longer Zacharias delayed his return the greater the apprehension grew. His eventual exit was met with an audible gasp of relief, followed by a universal intake of breath as they observed his unsettled state of agitation. He weakly lifted a trembling hand to ask for their attention. The company fell silent and Zacharias made as though to address the people. He opened his mouth to speak, but no words came past his lips. He could not utter a single word. He was visibly distressed. He was dumb!

His colleagues led Zacharias discreetly away from the public gaze whilst the people dispersed to discuss the strange behaviour of the priest. They escorted him to his home at Bet Hakerem where his anxious wife was the essence of patience as he tried by various means and signals to explain to her the happenings of the day. Her eyes opened wide with the realisation that her husband had actually communicated with an angelic visitor. Then came the news of the promise of a child. Amazingly she did not respond with doubt as her husband had done and as Sarah the famous mother of Israel had done in the past. Instead she began to laugh and shout with unbounded joy. Then she danced! She shouted! She sang! She gazed into her husband's bewildered eyes and spoke faith into his soul.

"Zacharias, we are going to have a son. I, Elizabeth, barren all my life, am going to bear a son in my old age! He will be a servant of the Lord, a forerunner of the Messiah. Zacharias, I am so happy, so blessed." She wept with unrestrained joy and her bemused husband beamed his silent approval.

They had been married for almost fifty years and were more in love now than they had ever been. Later that wonderful night they knelt together to thank God for his goodness. Then he took her in his arms and told her how much he loved her and how beautiful she was. Then they loved each other with all the passion of their youth and that night God opened up the womb of his faithful handmaiden and a child was conceived who was ordained in God's purposes from the beginning of time.

They lay together in each other's arms for a long time and Elizabeth talked of the wondrous revelation which the angel brought about the future of their son. He would turn many of his people to God. He was destined for greatness. Many would have good reason to thank God for the day of his birth.

"I wonder what he will do?" she smiled. "I wonder where he will go. I wonder why he will be called great."

Don't ask Elizabeth! Don't look beyond your revelation. You may see in the dark mists of future happenings that which you never need to see. You may catch a glimpse of a wild looking man in the wilderness of Judea. You may hear the howl of a mountain wind and feel the unwelcome chill of a prison cave. You may see the flash of a naked blade and behold the blood soaked head of a son still young.

CHAPTER THREE

The valley of Jezreel, a lush and fertile plain which spreads its mantle from the Mediterranean coast just north of modern day Haifa across to the Jordan valley in the east of Palestine, was Israel's natural divide between the province of Galilee to the north and Judea to the south. From the small stubby peninsula where Haifa now proudly sits there exists a range of hills which forms the southern border of the plain, beginning with Mount Carmel on the coast, sprawling south eastwards towards the southern hills of Samaria, then turning due south in a line parallel with the Jordan River to Jerusalem and beyond, as far as Hebron, west of the Dead Sea. This spine of hills was known in ancient times as "The Hill Country."

The many travellers who traversed the valley eastwards, following the northern bank of the River Kishon, left behind them on their right the impressive Mount Carmel, the scene of the prophet Elijah's famous victory over the prophets of Baal during the reign of King Ahab and his wicked queen, Jezebel. It was here that Elijah called the fire down from heaven upon a water-soaked altar in an unprecedented display of Divine power. Another five or six miles further, again on the right, was the historic city of Megiddo, where Barak defeated Sisera in the time of the prophetess Deborah and where good king Josiah was slain in a battle with Pharoah-necho, king of Egypt, his body being carried by chariot from Megiddo to Jerusalem for burial. Here of course, according to the prophets, will be the site for the final battle of history, when the nations are predicted to unite against Israel in the battle of Armageddon. Two or three more miles and they could see in the distance, in front but slightly to the north, the hill of Moreh where Gideon defeated the Midianites in battle with only three hundred men. To the southeast were the far-off contours of Mount Gilboa where Saul and his son Jonathan met their end in battle with the Philistines and upon which the great King David pronounced his curse in his anguished lament for his friends.

"Ye mountains of Gilboa," he cried with a wail of sorrow. "Let there be no dew, neither let there be rain, upon you, nor fields of offerings: for there the shield of the mighty is vilely cast away, the shield of Saul, as though he had not been anointed."

Many travellers would at this juncture head for Judea either by way of the Hill Country or by continuing eastwards with the intention of following the Jordan Valley southwards. Others turned north through a natural cleft in the limestone rock that gave exit from the plain and a passage through the foothills of the Lower Galilee. Such did not travel far before they engaged a most picturesque and verdant gorge, lush with greenery, which in summer months was splashed with divers colours from all manner of multicoloured wild flowers. Wild orchids struggled to be seen in the growth under trees and bushes and blue lupins boasted their colour against the carpets of wild mustard flowers. In the winter months this same ravine became a natural vortex for an unwelcoming chill wind as it sought exit from the plain. The passage widened as it ascended until it opened up into a large basin surrounded by hills, almost as though nature had designed her own amphitheatre and hidden it between the fifteen hills which encircled the site, the highest rising to a height of six hundred feet. Here, nestling incognito from the outside world was the city of Nazareth, lying like a babe in the cradle of the grass carpeted hills. Saint Jerome compared this city to the opening of a rose, describing it as "the flower of Galilee."

It does seem ironic that a city built in such a beautiful and spectacular setting was the despised of the despised. The more cultured people of the south scorned the whole province of Galilee. It was prejudicially known as "Galilee of the Gentiles" because of its cosmopolitan population. Phoenicians, Arabs, Greeks, as well as Jews, inhabited its towns and villages, and the dialect was far less polished than that of Judea. For an unknown reason which is lost to the pages of history the city of Nazareth was despised even by the residents of Galilee. Indeed, it was a native of Galilee who posed the very revealing question, "Can any good thing come out of Nazareth?" The reason for such a parochial attitude is a matter for speculation, especially in consideration of the outstanding geographical beauty of the place. What evil may have been promoted there, what civil disobedience, religious illegality, or grievous moral diversity, nobody knows. What is certain, however, is that this most contemned community in the whole of Israel was, in the providence and purposes of a God who delights to take the weak and base and foolish things of this world to confound the mighty, the town chosen to be the home town of One who would change the history of the world.

CHAPTER FOUR

It was a hot summer's day in mid-August and Nazareth was baking in the afternoon sun. A young girl was climbing the hill to the west of the city, pausing occasionally to look back at the town below. Heat haze rose like candescent mist from the sweating flat-roofed houses, each one transfigured into a mirror by the sun, producing scores of shimmering lights in the brightness of the day. An eagle startled her as it swooped over her head and glided majestically across the sleepy habitat to the grassy slopes beyond. She stood for a moment to absorb the scene before continuing her ascent. She was only fifteen years of age and her trim but mature figure belied the hidden strength accrued by much hard work, work that was the natural inheritance of a Jewish girl born into abject poverty. She navigated the rising terrain with the agility of a young hind and was soon standing triumphantly at the summit, pirouetting impressively on her toes as though speed reading the wondrous panorama which her vantage point afforded her. Her large hazel coloured eyes, normally dark peaceful pools of tranquillity, were alive and sparkling with excitement. Her brown face, bronzed with daily exposure to the summer sun, was flushed with radiant happiness. She tossed her ample black tresses to the warm wind which repetitively swept in huge ripples across the grassy heights and laughed aloud as they blew back, wrapping themselves around her face. She was deliriously happy. She was happier than she had ever been in her whole life. Her heart was pounding with the unspeakable exhilaration of true love. Mary, youngest daughter of the late Heli and

Ann, born in the lineage of the great King David, was hopelessly in love. She had lost her heart to the kindest, sweetest, most gentle and honourable man and in her view the most amazingly handsome man, in the whole of Israel. She had loved him from a distance for many weeks, but today she had discovered that her love was requited. She now knew that he loved her in return and her heart was bathing in the deep, pure joy of love. She lifted her head to the heavens as though allowing the angels to gaze upon her contentment.

Her features were too strong to be classed as pretty, but her inherited high cheekbones, a proud nose and crystal clear eyes, claimed a unique attractiveness of their own. Her long hair shone like the feathers of a blackbird. She was simply dressed in a light cotton dress and she carried her sandals in her hand. She loved to run barefoot through the soft grass. She loved the feeling of freedom. How free she felt on this wonderful day! She ran down the steep slope into the wind and felt her hair lifting up behind her, like she was flying, free of the troubles and encumbrances of life. She called to the birds that wheeled above her. She shouted her message into time and it floated over the hills to infinity.
"I love you Joseph," she shouted. "I love you forever."
She dropped her sandals into the grass and wrapped her arms around herself, right hand on her left hip, left hand on her right, and feigned a shiver in the sunshine.

Joseph, son of Jacob, was a carpenter in Nazareth. That in no way indicated prosperity for he was in fact a poor man. In another culture and another time his expertise in the craft of woodwork would have made him financially secure, especially as he was not only a skilled builder and repairer of roofs, but also a workman of no mean ability in the art of fine furniture making and other more intricate woodwork, but in the Jewish culture of his time the public use of his skills was regarded as almost a religious duty and brought him only small remuneration. He was a hard-working man nevertheless and a widower despite being only twenty-seven years of age. He tragically lost his beloved wife in childbirth and was now struggling to bring up his five young children alone. They were three boys, Justus aged ten, Simon aged nine, Judas aged seven, and two girls, Esther aged five and Tamar aged two. The children missed their mother desperately and depended on their devoted father for everything. Father and children were bound together in deepest love, a bond made more powerful by their shared grief. Joseph was universally respected both as a father and as a man of upright character and honour.

He was a regular attendee at the local Synagogue and his love for God was without doubt the controlling influence of his life. His understanding of the scriptures inspired within him a deep and fervent anticipation of the coming of the long awaited Messiah. He was occasionally privileged to be chosen as one of the men to mount the 'Bema' in the centre of the Synagogue upon which rested the 'Luach' or lectern upon which was placed the sacred scroll. Here he would read from the Law of Moses or from the Prophets. It was on one such occasion of recent weeks when, having completed his reading, as he stepped down to return to his seat, he happened to glance up into the balcony where the women of Nazareth sat during the often protracted service.

In doing so he caught the eye of a young woman who was gazing at him with unabashed admiration. She quickly lowered her eyes and a blush of embarrassment reddened her cheeks. The incident lasted for only a moment, but spoke volumes. Unknown to Joseph the young girl, Mary, had been secretly admiring him for weeks, choosing to quietly and discreetly bear her burden of love.

The following Sabbath Joseph found himself unconsciously scanning the faces of the assembled women in search of the girl and again their eyes met, this time for several seconds and the suggestion of a smile passed between them. Throughout the duration of the lengthy service that Sabbath morning Joseph cast repeated glances in the direction of his admirer, marvelling at her rapt attention to all that was going on. Her lips often moved in silent unison with the 'Sheliach Tsibbur' as he read the prayers, and responded 'Amen' at the conclusion of the three sections of the priestly blessing. It was obvious that she was no mere religious spectator. Her mouth mimed many of the readings and she drank in the sermons with genuine spiritual enthusiasm. For a young teenage girl she manifested an unusual appetite for Godly matters. Joseph was intrigued.

The Jewish custom of hastening to the Synagogue for the service, but leaving it more slowly, symbolising an eagerness to approach God and a reluctance to depart his presence, suited the cause of the carpenter well that Sabbath morn. He dallied with intent just outside the door, hoping for a chance meeting with the girl in the balcony, but was disappointed to see her pass by in deep conversation with a group of friends without even noticing him. He felt strangely sad and somewhat frustrated that he now must wait another whole week before he could see her again.

Mary felt irresistibly drawn to the vicinity of the carpenter's shop in the hope of catching a glimpse of the man who had captured her heart, but each time she yielded to her desire she drew a blank. The door always seemed closed and the only satisfaction which she gained was from knowing that she was so close, just a wall separating her from him. The exchange of smiles in the Synagogue served only to add fuel to the fire of her growing passion to meet him and she felt daily more magnetised to the carpentry. The compulsion grew until, now dominated by the power of love, she decided to present herself at Joseph's door. She had no idea what she was going to say or how she would conduct the interview. She felt foolish and embarrassed, but she went nevertheless, wending her way through the narrow streets until she arrived at the heavy wooden door of Joseph's workshop. She was wearing her prettiest dress and her hair was shining after vigorous brushing. Her heart pounded nervously as she knocked gently, hesitated for a moment, and then slowly pushed open the door. Joseph was leaning over his bench in the process of carving a piece of olive wood. He looked up to identify his visitor and as recognition dawned he stepped back with surprise. The sight of Mary caught him completely off guard and a mixture of shock, nervousness and delight lit up his face. Within seconds he relaxed into a pleasant smile of welcome.
"Please come in!" he said kindly. "I remember you from the Synagogue."

"Thank you."

She sat down shyly on one of a number of new chairs that were waiting for collection. She looked up and smiled. She was lost for words. Her eyes were a mixture of brown and green, soft like velvet, betraying a meekness of soul and perhaps a hint of sadness. Her sweet and pure spirit was her major attractiveness and Joseph felt himself instantly yearning to touch her soul. They sat for several seconds searching each other's eyes, neither of them offering to break the spell. She thought he looked weary, probably from overwork and she noticed how his strong hands were rough from handling the timber. She knew of his bereavement and her heart was touched with compassion for both him and his children. To be widowed at such a young age was pain enough, but to have the responsibility of five young children whilst trying to run a business was, in her estimation, too much for any man. She wanted to help him. She had a genuine desire to minister to this man's children and to give them comfort in their loss. Her feelings in the silence were all selfless, a powerful, present evidence of the future sacrificial love which was to characterise her life.

Her embarrassment and nervousness faded with the passing moments. She felt at home in the same room as this wonderful man. He was of average height and build and his face was kind. His strong, handsome features were enhanced by his closely trimmed beard and his eyes shone like water sparkling in the sunshine.

"I just came…." Her voice faltered and the sentence died. Then, after a pause, "I just came to see you."

Joseph smiled his response and she smiled coyly in return.

"Do you attend the Synagogue every week?" he asked.

It was the trigger which launched Mary into her favourite subject.

"Oh yes, Joseph!" She sat erect in her chair, her back straight, her head uplifted, her hair pushed back over her narrow shoulders and her dark eyes flashed with life.

"I love God with all my heart. He is the love of my life and I seek him daily in prayer and devotion. I know the scriptures, the law and the prophets, and I love to attend the Sabbath services, to hear the preaching and join in the prayers to Jehovah. Is not God so wonderful Joseph? Soon he will send our Messiah and all Israel will be saved from oppression and he will fulfil his promise to our fathers, Abraham, Isaac, and Jacob."

Joseph smiled broadly at such a genuine outburst of love for the Almighty. Rarely had he seen such passion for God in one so young and his spirit blended with hers in a common commitment to the God of Israel. He thought how beautiful she was, how pure and innocent her large transparent eyes and what a humble attitude exuded from her life.

The two of them talked about God and history and the future of Israel for more than an hour, during which Mary displayed a high intellect and an outstanding knowledge of a cross section of subjects. If Joseph had not already lost his heart to this girl in the Synagogue a few days earlier he certainly lost it now. He was destined to love her for the rest of his life.

"I would very much like to meet your children, Joseph, if you do not think me too forward in asking?"
"Of course not," he replied eagerly. "Perhaps you would like to come and share our Sabbath meal with us after the service on Saturday. You could meet the children and we could spend the afternoon together."
She happily agreed and Joseph politely accompanied her to the door. She stepped outside into the hot afternoon sunshine and as she glanced back to smile farewell their eyes met once more and in the lingering exchange two human spirits embraced at the very deepest level and heaven clapped its hands. In that moment Mary knew that she was in love and she knew that he loved her also. Her heart was dancing as she made her way alone to climb her favourite hill.

CHAPTER FIVE

During the following weeks Mary became a regular visitor to the home of Joseph and his family. The workshop was part of their dwelling, the whole of which was universally known as "The Carpentry." The children were boisterous but loveable and quickly related to Mary's youthful approach. She told them stories, most of them from the scriptures, and they thrilled at her accounts of the miraculous opening of the Red Sea, Samson and the lion, David and Goliath and many others. Some days Mary went to the house while Joseph was at work and prepared the evening meal and on other days she washed the children's clothes. She demonstrated her love in the only way true love is ever demonstrated, by her actions, and in so doing the love between Joseph and her grew deeper. Often in the cool of the evening they walked together up Mary's favourite hill to admire the scenery in the crimson glow of the setting sun. It was a pleasant walk from the town, past the olive grove where the fruit was beginning to turn purple ready for harvesting, past the pomegranate trees clothed with their dark green foliage, the fruit turning red in preparation for gathering in mid-October. Then came the grassy slopes and the tall palm tree which stood impressively like a guard at the edge of town, a proud forty feet tall, with huge emerald green plumes, like ostrich feathers whispering in the breeze. The view from the hill was amazing. To the west they could see Mount Carmel and on a clear evening the Great Sea beyond, a distant red pool swallowing the dying sun. To the east they could see the peaceful outline of the beautiful Mount Tabor and to the north the plateaus of Zebulun and Naphtali with the distant outline of the magnificent Mount Hermon which in a few months time would be carrying its winter crown of glistening snow. To the south lay the sprawling plain of Jezreel. The young couple stood together and pointed at the scenes of differing beauty. They talked of the Creator, marvelling at his workmanship, grateful that He gave this land of "milk and honey" to the descendants of Abraham. Then they descended the hill to the north west of the city until they reached the town well which was a popular meeting point for the local women as well as a resting place for many a weary traveller. They spent many hours here at the close of the day and told each other secrets and talked of undying love.

Late summer gave way to autumn and the failing sap contrived a beauty in the face of death, turning leaves into golden brown and mixing their colour with the persistent greenery of the myrtle, juniper and box trees. The mountains were clad with a patchwork of orange, pink and yellow, a breathtaking garden of leaves. The days grew shorter and soon the ice-cold chill of winter drove the couple from their mountain trysting place to the warm interior of Joseph's home and the heat-belching wood stove which was fed with endless supplies of sweet smelling off-cuts from the workshop. It was here, on a cold night in late November, that Joseph asked Mary to marry him. In a few weeks she was to be sixteen years of age and he would be most honoured if on that special day she would become his espoused wife. She was ecstatic with love and excitement. She had prayed for so much to Jehovah that he would grant to her this man to be her husband and how she praised and thanked him that wonderful night for the answer to her prayers.

Engagement in Israel, which could last for as long as one year before the actual marriage took place, was as binding as the marriage itself. Any breach of faithfulness in the relationship was regarded as adultery and the arrangement could only be terminated by a legal divorce. The engagement ceremony was an official occasion during which vows were exchanged in the presence of witnesses and at the conclusion a special prayer of benediction was pronounced. The happy couple then drank in turn from a single glass of wine to celebrate and demonstrate their pledged union. There was of course no physical union until such time as they were married.

So it was that upon the occasion of her sixteenth birthday Mary pledged herself to Joseph with all her heart, promising that on a day to be arranged she would become his wife. They stood and faced each other with mutual respect and with hands joined in a symbol of their united hearts they looked into each other's souls and made their vows the one to the other. Neither of them had any idea that this was no chance occurrence. They were enacting a scene which was ordained from the foundations of the world, for these two young people, both of whom were descendants of King David, were chosen by Almighty God himself to be the guardians of his Son, God clothed in human flesh.

The arrival of January brought no respite from the cold weather and it was on a particularly bitterly hostile night that Mary retired early to her bed, not so much from tiredness as from a desire to keep warm. She had lived alone since the death of her parents in the little house which she had always known as home. She missed them very much, especially on nights like this and she missed her sister Salome who was now married and living in Bethsaida by the lake. She was very much in love with Joseph and was unashamedly and with great enthusiasm anticipating her wedding day, but she never forgot the first love of her life, the God of Israel and it was in her relationship with Him that she found refuge in her loneliness. It was her custom to read a passage from the scriptures each night before settling down to sleep and her reading that night happened to be from the book of the prophet Isaiah and concerned the One who was prophesied to appear one day as the future deliverer of Israel. The section which described the sufferings of the much awaited Messiah intrigued her a great deal. She could not understand how it could be that One so great could suffer as described. She read the words over and over, "He was wounded for our transgressions, He was bruised for our iniquities: the chastisement of our peace was upon Him; and with His stripes we are healed …. He is brought as a lamb to the slaughter …. He was taken from prison and from judgement ….. He was cut off out of the land of the living: for the transgression of my people was He stricken." The words made no sense to her. How could the promised future king of Israel possibly suffer and die? Yet she felt strangely affected by the words, apprehensive, perhaps even a little afraid. They made her feel like weeping. Her belly knotted, like some unseen hand twisted her inside. She felt somehow involved in this imperceptible suffering of another. She shivered, closed the book, and snuffed out her candle. She whispered, "I love you" into her pillow, to Joseph and her Lord, and closed her eyes for sleep.

Whether she actually fell asleep or not she never really knew, but she was suddenly wide awake, her heart pounding against her rib cage. Someone was in her room! She could feel somebody there although the moonlight which crept defiantly through the gaps in the crudely constructed shutters revealed no one. She tried to stem the flow of adrenaline which surged through her veins. She was afraid but subdued the urge to scream. She slowly lifted herself up onto her elbows and peered into the half-light straining her ears to listen. The awareness of another presence in the room evolved in intensity by the second, but simultaneously her apprehension diminished and was replaced with an overwhelming sensation of awe. On several occasions in her life she had felt the presence of God when she prayed and she now became conscious that it was that kind of an aura, something beautiful and supernatural, which filled her room. The feeling was more powerful than anything she had known in the past and it became more so as she waited. She gasped as the room was flooded with a wonderful atmosphere of holiness. A soft, delicate light illuminated her simple chamber and with it came serene warmth like the caress of the morning summer sun. Mary rolled away from her sleeping mat and assumed a kneeling position in the centre of the floor. She began to whisper a psalm of worship, but her voice was instantly eclipsed by the sonorous tones of the most amazing voice she had ever heard. It was quite audible. Its origin was from someone or something in her room and it was calling her by her name. She opened her eyes to search for the owner of the voice and there before her, standing in her poor and humble bedchamber, unfazed by her obvious low estate, was a visitor from another realm, resplendent, magnificent and glorious. She was mute with wonderment. The spectre was one of unparalleled beauty, a vision of serene dignity. There stood before her one after the similitude of a man: tall, strong, and breathtakingly handsome. His visage was perfectly featured, like sculptured marble; his lips were full and his hair as black as pitch. His eyes were beyond anything she had ever imagined. They were marine blue and radiated a translucent, searching purity, as though they had the power to discern and cleanse. From his wide shoulders and resting caressingly over his arms and hands there tapered to his waist a pair of wings, luminous with inherent light. She had read of flying angels and of cherubim with wings and had always imagined that they must look quite strange, particularly when associated with the male form, but the wings on this phenomenal creature, though they appeared as fragile and delicate as silk, seemed so natural and far from looking out of place, actually enhanced his aura of power. A girdle of ornate gold ennobled a tunic of the same colour which fell in length to midway between his waist and knees, revealing strong, masculine thighs, like those of a toned athlete. His feet were bare albeit unsullied by any journey he may have travelled. His whole countenance was compelling, gentle but powerful, graceful but authoritative. Mary was utterly captivated, fascinated, breathless, altogether entranced by the apparition before her. Her instincts told her that she should prostrate herself before such an obvious dignitary yet she found herself incapable of diverting her gaze from the alluring eyes of her visitor. Then he spoke again, quietly but with an authority which penetrated her spirit.

"Hail, thou that art highly favoured, the Lord is with thee: blessed art thou among women."

Mary was visibly troubled at his words and a different kind of fear prodded at her inside. Sensing her trepidation he continued, "Fear not Mary: for thou hast found favour with God. And behold thou shalt conceive in thy womb, and bring forth a son, and shall call his name Jesus. He shall be great, and shall be called the Son of the Highest: and the Lord God shall give unto him the throne of his father David: And he shall reign over the house of Jacob for ever; and of his kingdom there shall be no end."

For the first time Mary ventured to speak to the angel. The words struggled to escape the constriction in her throat and her voice trembled with emotion.

"How shall these things be, seeing I know not a man?"

It was as though the staggering import of the promised child's identity was lost in the ridiculous impossibility of being told that she was to bear a child without the involvement of a man. She knew that this was impossible. Her question was most reasonable.

"The Holy Ghost shall come upon thee, and the power of the Highest shall overshadow thee: therefore also that holy thing that shall be born of thee shall be called the Son of God. And, behold, thy cousin Elizabeth, she also hath conceived a son in her old age: and this is the sixth month with her who was called barren. For with God nothing shall be impossible."

Mary understood the words. This angelic being was informing her that in some supernatural way God himself would replace the role of the man and be the father of her child and that she, a virgin, would bring forth a child. It was all so preposterous, yet the atmosphere in her room was pregnant with such energy, such authority, such a burning sense of truth, that she could do nothing but submit. It was, however, a matter for the willing surrender of her will, as it is with all who are challenged to commit to the Divine will at cost to themselves, but her choice was made. She heard herself saying, "Behold the handmaid of the Lord; be it unto me according to thy word."

Her head was bowed in reverent acquiescence and when she raised it again the vision had departed and her room was empty. The light and the warmth were gone and the cold chill of night was back in the air and driving her back beneath the covers. She lay awake for a long time replaying the strange visitation over and over in her mind. Dawn was breaking before she finally fell into a fitful sleep. She dreamed that she was with child and enduring the pangs of labour. She tossed around on her sleeping mat as surges of phantom pain swept through her brain and turned a dream into a nightmare. A huge dragon-like creature with mucous dribbling from its fiery jaws was crouched between her legs hungrily waiting to devour her child at the moment of its birth. She could see the detail of the slimy scales contorting with the movement of the beast and she could feel the heat of its foul breath against her thighs. She screamed with the contractions which tore at her stomach and for fear of the fiend and her screams jolted her into consciousness. The winter sun was streaming in through the ill-fitting shutters.

At that moment the reality of the dream appeared more real than the visit of the angel. Indeed the glorious visitor of the night seemed a mere fiction, an actor in a dream long passed. She lay anxiously contemplating the events of preceding hours. Had there really been an angel in her room? If so, had he actually told her that she would be with child by the Holy Ghost? She could clearly remember many of the words he had spoken to her, but she could also remember the details on the snout of the monster who had assailed her in her dream. How could she be sure that one was a dream and the other not? Perhaps the whole night was a figment of her imagination. Perhaps her mind was overactive, her emotions too fanciful. Maybe all these thoughts of love and marriage coupled with her deep love for God and her belief in the coming Messiah had combined to deceive her mind and produce weird visions of angels. She dressed slowly, pensive and deep in contemplation and shuddered at the image of the dragon which was indelibly imprinted on her mind. She wondered if it was possible that her cousin Elizabeth was pregnant. That would be something of a sign to her and a confirmation of the angel's words, but she lived much too far away for it to be confirmed one way or the other. She wanted to talk to Joseph about the experiences of the night but how could she tell her future husband that she had been visited by an angel who told her that she was going to have a baby without intimately knowing a man? He was a believer and loved God dearly, but such an account would more than challenge his capacity to believe. She decided to dismiss the incident from her mind, or at least make an attempt to do so.

It was a more subdued Mary who went about her duties that day and she was somewhat thankful that Joseph had a busy day at work. She wanted to see him, but was relieved that she did not, for any encounter would have necessitated either telling him her absurd story or enduring the tension of avoiding doing so. So the day dragged on, each hour seeming like two, until darkness once more shrouded the city of Nazareth. She discovered that she was more than a little timorous about going to her bed.

CHAPTER SIX

It was a confused and bewildered teenager who knelt to pray in her bare cold room that lonely night. She clutched her threadbare woollen shawl around her slim form for warmth and pensively scrutinised the corner of the room where the angel appeared the previous night. All was silent and still, but she was loath to settle down to sleep for fear that she would dream again of the dragon. She could still envisage the small evil eyes of the scaly monster and a sensation of cold fear coursed its way down her spine. She lifted her eyes heavenward and began to pray.
"Oh God of Abraham, Isaac, and Jacob, Almighty and holy, I love you."
With the expression of adoration her fear and loneliness took flight and the warmth of love spread sweetly through her heart. Enjoying an increasing sense of peace she gently lifted her hands and continued her prayer.
"I yield myself to you, all I have and all I am, to do your will, to spend my life, whatever the cost, in your great service. Use me Lord of heaven and earth, use me in whatever way pleases You. Cleanse me from my sin, from every hidden fault and weakness, and always hear me when I call to You."
She began to recite the psalm of repentance written by King David after his shameful act of adultery with Bathsheba, wife of Uriah the Hittite. She knew the psalm well having committed it to memory as a child and having made it her own prayer on numerous occasions. She was fully aware of her weaknesses and sincerely mourned when she felt that she displeased her Lord. She prayed it now.

"Have mercy upon me, O God, according to thy loving kindness …. Cleanse me from my sin …. Wash me and I shall be whiter than snow …. Create in me a clean heart, O God, and renew a right spirit within me …. Uphold me with thy free spirit."

She felt better having prayed. She could trust the God of her fathers. Had He not proved Himself so many times throughout the history of His people? Had He not been with Esther in the harem of King Ahasuerus and comforted her on the lonely nights she cried herself to sleep? Had He not planned that she be made queen in order to save her people from the wicked scheme of Haman? Surely the God of Esther was her God also and would preserve her safe through the dark hours of the night to the blessings of a new day. She laid herself down in peace and with a rationale of wellbeing based on her belief that God was with her. For a fleeting moment she thought of the dragon but the words of the psalmist flowed into her mind in an instant, "Thou shalt not be afraid of the terror by night." She sighed with thankfulness, smiled in the candlelight, and closed her eyes.

Suddenly it seemed as though she could see through the flat roof of her little home into the night sky beyond. It appeared that, just above her house, she could see a cloud of light, brighter at its centre and paling somewhat at its periphery, burning but not moving, beautiful but powerful. There was no figure, no angel, just the most divine light one could ever imagine, bright but not offensive to her vision. She opened her eyes but she could still see it. She then experienced an indescribable yearning to climb inside the awesome presence which she felt the flame represented. Her soul reached for it like a child for its mother but she lay quite still and made no attempt to rise. Tears of adoration slowly trickled from her eyes. Then she saw beyond the light a whirling mass of darkness silhouetted against the star-lit sky, a darkness that she could feel. It was moving and swirling like an angry storm cloud posturing to destroy, agitated to place itself between the flame of light and Mary's room. In the centre of the vortex she could make out the twisted snout of the dragon with its bloodshot eyes and snarling visage. It was roaring but she could hear no sound. She felt no fear for she was possessed of a confidence that the darkness was incapable of overcoming the light. She watched and waited as the black cloud and its evil occupant made salvo after salvo against the holy flame but all to no avail, until suddenly the light divided and swallowed up the darkness and in an instant it was gone. Mary laughed aloud at the victory but then felt a little foolish for her wild imaginings. She once again closed her eyes for sleep, the hint of a smile adorning her youthful lips.

There was to be no sleep, however, for now the living flame was in her room, a blaze of light as bright as the noonday sun filled her bed chamber and with it came an atmosphere so charged with supernatural power that she gasped with awe. She looked for no angel because she instinctively knew that this presence was beyond the angelic. This was the essence of Divinity, the 'Shekinah Glory' which had first filled the holy Tabernacle in the wilderness in the days of Moses and rested thereafter upon the sacred Ark of the Covenant. The invisible Spirit of Almighty God was in her room and she dared not move or venture to speak. Tears flowed, tears of utter wonderment and joy. Her face glowed with a radiance never seen on earth since the face of Moses shone with similar luminescence after his meeting with God on the holy mount. She drew in her breath as the presence became more intense and she trembled at the touch of the Eternal One. Infinity caressed the finite and the immortal God blended with mortality. The creator embraced his creation and from the crown of her head to the tips of her toes there flowed the fire of eternal life. Every fibre of her being was saturated with the power of the Holy Spirit as an overwhelming ecstasy beyond description swept her human form. She bathed in the fountain of light as the fullness of the Godhead overshadowed the yielded body of his handmaiden. Wave after wave of immeasurable glory pulsated through her being and the words of the archangel Gabriel echoed in her mind, "That holy thing which shall be born of thee shall be called the Son of God." She heard the sound of the Glory of God, like the ocean crashing against the age worn rocks on the shores of the Great Sea. Lightening flashed across the clear night sky and thunder rolled in distant voids. For a moment, only for a moment, she saw through the firmament of the heavens the opening of a huge curtain and through it stepped One of purest holiness, His eyes like flaming fire. He was clothed with a full length robe and about His chest was a golden girdle. His hair was as white as lamb's wool and His feet like burnished brass. Protruding from His mouth was a glittering two-edged sword and His countenance shone like the morning sun. The curtain closed behind Him and He stepped into her room. The Messiah!

Then it was over. Mary and her room were left with a lingering sense of unspeakable peace. The light itself was gone but the candles were still redundant in its aftermath. On this most sacred night, in fulfilment of the word of the angel, God had visited His willing servant and planted within her womb the embodiment of Himself. She enjoyed a calm and growing confidence that whatever the future held she could trust the One who had visited her and she knew that whatever He did would be right. Her fingers nervously touched the smooth surface of her flat belly. Could this really be? What miracle was now enacting beneath that veil of human flesh. Was the child of Elohim already beginning to grow within her womb? Was the majestic Christ she had witnessed stepping through heaven's curtain now a mere seed within her maiden form?

"I love you Lord," she whispered, and her eyes were following the movement of her hands. A moments pause, and then she said, "Love of my life."

CHAPTER SEVEN

The morning light cast a strange shadow of unreality across the amazing happenings of the night. It could not rob her of the memory of the undoubted presence of God which visited her in her room, but it did steal away some of Mary's assurance that the visitation was definitely linked with the promise of the angel on the previous night. She found that in the normality of a new day impossibility became more powerful and inevitably rose to contest the annunciation of the angel, not that she ceased to believe, but she experienced an unsettling of her spirit. Doubt in some measure definitely played a part in her considerations concerning what to tell Joseph. She really needed to talk to him but reckoned it impossible. She reasoned that there was absolutely no way that he could even begin to understand. Without the intervention of doubt she would have realised that there was no alternative but to share with him the events of the last two nights, but she concluded that wisdom required silence, a silence which left matters in the hands of God and to the unfolding of time. So Mary attempted to put the events of the past few days out of her mind and sought to carry on with life as normal. Within a couple of days she was back to her old self, laughing and talking with Joseph, playing with the children, and busying herself with making life a little easier for others.

Weeks passed and Mary's cycle was due to produce her monthly issue. None came. She subdued an emotional mix of excitement and apprehension, reminding herself that she had been late before. She knew deep down that she would be disappointed if she was not with child, yet she was most anxious about the consequences if she was. Weeks passed and she felt strangely different. Moments of nausea swept over her and she had strange, tingling sensations in her breasts. Her body felt different and a strong call of destiny flooded her soul. Again the words of the angel echoed and re-echoed in her mind, "That holy thing that shall be born of thee shall be called the Son of God." She raised her eyes, misty with emotion, and searched the heavens for help. She had never physically known a man, yet she was pregnant. Who was this Son of God within her virgin womb? What divine council had predestined her for such a role as this? What would become of her in a hostile environment, in a culture which would consider her a lawbreaker, and what would become of the child she would bring forth? He would be called the bastard son of an immoral woman. She cringed at the prospect of coming misunderstanding and persecution.

She stood alone and naked in her chamber and ran her hands again and again over her stomach, as though caressing the unknown, touching the flesh beneath which grew the embodiment of God. It was bizarre, irrational, absurd and unbelievable, but it was true. The Spirit of the God of Israel, the Almighty 'I am', had stepped into the tiny vestibule within the body of a teenage girl and would emerge as God clothed with human flesh.

Mary's unreserved acceptance of the reality of her pregnancy brought with it the daunting, but now unavoidable prospect of attempting to explain the inexplicable to her fiancé. She walked the hilly slopes she had traversed a hundred times before and rehearsed aloud the speech she had prepared for her beloved. She would tell him first about the night the angel came to her room and all that he had said to her. Then she would describe to the best of her ability the occurrences of that holy night the Lord visited her and baptised her in His presence, how He planted within her womb the holy seed. She would tell him how she had waited for the evidence of the miracle before speaking to him about it, and how she was now with child. She envisaged him standing before her and imagined his response. She saw the look of shock and horror on his weary face, the unbelief behind his sorrowing eyes, and she felt the agony of his injured soul. She heard his breaking voice ask her why she never told him of the angel's visit at the time. She felt the pain of the searing hurt which would tear at his betrayed heart, heard his stern request for truth and his demand for the identity of her lover. Whichever way she practised her defence, or however much she pleaded for his listening ear, she heard the same reply and felt the same unavoidable rejection. She knew that he would not believe, indeed could not believe, for nothing after this fashion had ever happened before. She was fully aware that her speech sounded ridiculous. She searched the skies for an answer and turned her heart in supplication to the God she loved.

"Oh God, if he must understand this mystery, then you must make him understand, for I am sure no words of mine will ever give him peace."

Mary revived her failing courage and with a heart heavy with anxiety made her familiar journey to Joseph's door. He welcomed her with eyes filled with gentleness and love, but was instantly concerned at the obvious look of apprehension which lined the face of his betrothed. She did not delay the agony but, taking his rugged hands within her own, gazed beseechingly into his puzzled eyes. She then falteringly pronounced her defence. The response was exactly as she anticipated. He demonstrated no anger, for such was not his nature, but he was obviously deeply grieved. He posed the questions which she anticipated he would ask and she answered them with truth. Unfortunately it was truth which was considerably stranger than fiction and would have no positive effect. How she wished now that she had told him of the angel's visit the very next morning and prepared him for all of this. She pleaded and she wept but it availed nothing. Her story was preposterous. He viewed her as a guilty party who in her desperation had succeeded in convincing herself of some divine participation in her crime. It was an absurd and futile ploy to escape the consequences of her sin. His love for Mary was beyond question and he felt not the slightest desire for revenge. There was no instinct to publicly humiliate her or cause her to fall foul of the law, but his position was untenable. He could not possibly continue his engagement in these circumstances so he had no alternative but to break his espousal as privately and discreetly as possible. He informed her that he would give careful thought as to how to proceed and escorted her politely to the door. She took a few steps into the cold, evening air and stumbled under her heavy load of love and despair. She looked back through tears of anguish into the face of the man she loved. His face was contorted with inconsolable grief. Tears were flowing freely into his beard. He was like a bereaved man, void of hope. Their mutual pain was unbearable.

Every step towards her home was a step of thrilling agony. She felt so completely alone. A frustrated yearning to be believed filled her throat with vomit. Her legs collapsed under her and she fell in a heap in the dust of the road. She staggered to her feet and with the gait of a drunkard stumbled to her door, entered, and locked it behind her. Within seconds she was prostrate on the floor and sobbing uncontrollably into her pillow. What could she possibly do?

Joseph, her own beloved Joseph, was lost to her, believing her to be nothing better than an adulteress, an immoral betrayer of both man and God. She was alone in the world, irrevocably trapped in circumstances which no other human being on earth would believe. She spent the night drowning in an unfathomable lake of sleepless despair waiting forever for the postponed dawn. She could no longer stay in Nazareth, yet she had nowhere else to go. She refused the temptation to run to her sister Salome and invade her happiness, but leave she must, and leave she would. With the first paling of the eastern sky she dressed in the warmest clothes that she possessed and stepped out into a cold February morning. A cold mist was rolling down her mountain as she clutched her ragged shawl about her trembling body and, carrying a small bag of essentials, made her way southward. The streets of Nazareth were deserted and a cold wind was blowing from the north against her back as she navigated the narrow streets, passed Joseph's carpentry with tears streaming down her face, and headed down the craggy incline towards Jezreel. It was a long walk to the city, but she knew that there she would be able to join herself to a caravan heading south through the hill country towards the city of Jerusalem. It was then that the inspiration came. Once again it was the memory of the words of the angel echoing in her memory which rescued her. The oration of the angel had declared "Thy cousin Elizabeth, she hath also conceived a son in her old age, and this is the sixth month with her, who was called barren." In an instant she knew what she should do. She would take the journey south and find her cousin. If there was a person alive on the planet who would understand it had to be her. Her footfall was a little lighter and her pace somewhat quicker as she headed down the valley towards Jezreel.

CHAPTER EIGHT

As the weeks passed into months Elizabeth and Zacharias pondered and communicated a great deal about the miracle child they were expecting. The full importance of the angel's words at the altar of incense seemed more significant as time passed and brought with them a developing sense of responsibility. Elizabeth increasingly felt the burden of her calling to be the mother of the forerunner of the Christ and the manifold and complex instructions already given for the upbringing of her child. The angel had told her husband that their son should never take strong drink nor cut his hair. He was to be after the order of the Nazarites who wore their hair long as a mark of their separation to God's service and of their willingness to suffer reproach for His Name. The angel furthermore declared that John would be of the same spirit as the great prophet Elijah who famously ascended to heaven in a whirlwind. He was to be a preacher of passionate disposition whose vocation was to urge people to prepare for the emergence of the Messiah. She did not broadcast her wonderful secret, choosing rather to adopt a more clandestine way of life away from public gaze. She did, however, rejoice greatly at the lifting of her reproach of infertility. At first it was difficult to cope with Zacharias' loss of speech but she gradually became accustomed to his silence, even joking that it had never been so peaceful. She prayed much for him and her unborn son.

She was six months into her pregnancy when she awoke one morning enveloped in an unusual ambiance of

anticipation. A profound awareness of God's presence permeated her home and her soul was inexplicably exulted. Zacharias was away in Jerusalem but she felt far from alone as she went about her daily chores. She had a song in her heart and a rising expectation in her spirit. She fell to musing concerning the coming Messiah. If the child that she was bearing was destined to prepare the way for the Christ, from whence would the latter come? Perhaps he was already born, or maybe he would be younger than her child. The prophet of old said that a virgin would conceive and bear a son and that his name would be called 'Emmanuel', meaning 'God with us'. What extraordinary and mysterious days these were. Could it be that at the very time when Roman legions oppressed her beloved Israel the Saviour of her people would be born? She began to vocalise her song and the sweet sound of her 'hallelujah's' filled her poor but well kept home. It was as though the music in her soul found unpremeditated expression on her yielded lips. Her spirit sang and her voice took up the strain. She was so lost in worship that she failed to hear the sound of footsteps on the gravel path outside her home, or the gentle tapping at her open door. She turned around in pursuit of her duties to discover a young maiden, smiling broadly, and standing at the threshold. For several seconds she peered into the face of her visitor in a search for recognition.
"It's me Elizabeth, Mary, your cousin from Nazareth."
Elizabeth squealed with delight and the two women fell weeping into each other's arms. She placed her hands softly on Mary's shoulders and eased her away in order to look more intently into her face. She opened her mouth to remark on how much she had changed since last they met, but was distracted by her baby kicking fiercely in her womb.

Then the presence of God which had so wonderfully filled her home that morning came upon her with overwhelming intensity. She began to utter words that were certainly beyond the capability of her own mind or intellect: God inspired words which bypassed her understanding. She was radiant, her eyes glowing with the life of a young woman as she verbalised the utterance of the Holy Spirit. She knew nothing of Mary's pregnancy and yet spoke of it with an authority and prophetic insight which is certain to remain on record until the end of time.
"Blessed art thou among women, and blessed is the fruit of thy womb. And whence is this to me, that the mother of my Lord should come to me? For, lo, as soon as the voice of thy salutation sounded in my ears, the babe leaped in my womb for joy. And blessed is she that believed: for there shall be a performance of those things which were told her from the Lord."

The last vestiges of doubt and fear that lurked in the heart of Mary were banished in an instant. The stress and worry of recent days, the weariness of her long journey, the severe emotional distress of losing Joseph, everything contrary to a feeling of wellbeing, was blown away like morning mist before the wind. It was all true. Nobody could doubt that, despite her age, Elizabeth was pregnant, just as the angel predicted, but to hear her cousin speaking so eloquently of her own invisible condition was to Mary an astonishing confirmation of the hand of God in her circumstances. Elizabeth could not possibly have foreknowledge of the child within her womb. Of course Mary believed before this, but now she believed at a new level and with renewed assurance. She now felt able to commit her whole circumstance, even the loss of Joseph, entirely and unreservedly to God. The burden lifted from her life and a joy unspeakable rose up within her soul. She wanted to shout, and sing, and dance, and give praise to God for the phenomenal privilege he had granted to one so unworthy. She laughed through her tears into the face of the aging Elizabeth and began her own inspired utterance of thanksgiving.

"My soul doth magnify the Lord, and my spirit hath rejoiced in God my Saviour. For he hath regarded the low estate of His handmaiden: for, behold, from henceforth all generations shall call me blessed. For He that is mighty hath done to me great things; and holy is His name. And His mercy is on them that fear Him from generation to generation."

She continued to praise God for His justice in exalting the lowly and bringing down the proud, and the two women bathed in the divine presence for a considerable time.

They talked for hours, exchanging experiences and sharing stories of angelic visitations and divine interventions in their lives. How awesome it was that the Almighty chose two cousins, one to bear the Messiah and the other, His forerunner, one of them pregnant by the Holy Spirit whilst still a virgin, the other pregnant by her husband when past child-bearing age. They speculated about the future and Mary confided some of her fears. She was no stranger to the writings of the prophets and continued to be perplexed by some of their utterances, especially some of Isaiah's predictions which seemed to indicate that Christ was to endure great suffering. The young mother-to-be was repulsed at the thought of her unborn child becoming the fulfilment of such prophecies. She gripped Elizabeth's hands and hoped for another explanation for the ancient writings but her cousin's eyes filled with tears and she lowered her head as though she also feared the unfolding years.

Mary wept as she told of her anguished separation from Joseph. Sobs convulsed her body as she spoke of his agony and hurt and of how he looked when she glanced back and saw him standing at his door. They prayed together that God would help him, even now, to understand. They also prayed for restoration of speech to Zacharias.

Mary settled well into the little house at Bet Hakerem, helping Elizabeth with her work as she became more heavily pregnant. The older woman struggled to cope with her burden. Her swollen breasts were paining her and her frail legs and back were aching under the increased load within her abdomen. The teenager was conscious of the divine hand upon both their lives as she helped her aged friend to endure the last few months of her pregnancy. How providential that the younger should help the elder and that the one whose son was destined to save the world should assist the mother of the one who would prepare the way before Him. Mary realised that Elizabeth could never have managed on her own. Maybe it was all in God's plan that Joseph was not told of the angel's visit, that he should refuse to believe, and that she should leave Nazareth. Perhaps the agony of her life these many weeks were all designed to provide Elizabeth with the help she needed. Despite her daily yearning for her lost love and the accompanying heartbreak it produced she was able to thank God for guiding her steps to this needy home. She remembered how, centuries before, Joseph, son of Jacob, had languished for years in the dungeon of Egypt but finally said, "It was God who sent me here." She was possessed of peace of soul that whispered, "All is well."

For three months Mary remained in the hill country, until the time came for Elizabeth to have her baby. She wanted to stay and help with the birth and she would have loved to have seen her cousin's miracle son, the boy who was given to play such a vital part in the purposes of God for her own unborn child, but she felt constrained to return to Nazareth. She tried to dismiss the pull of the place where her sadness rested, but the more she delayed the more powerful the compulsion became. A sense of urgency drove her to speak to Elizabeth. She explained how she felt and they agreed together that Mary should depart immediately for home. She bade a tearful farewell to her sister-friend, holding her full midriff between her open palms as a prayerful goodbye to the unborn child. It was agreed that Zacharias should escort her to the highway which ran north towards Jezreel and Elizabeth insisted that he must be careful to secure her a safe passage with bona fide pilgrims returning to Galilee. The old priest and his virgin charge picked their way down the rocky slope towards the road far below them. Mary turned and waved one final time and as Elizabeth wearily raised her hand in reply a strange involuntary tightening of her stomach muscles dragged at her middle. She quickly turned into her home. It had begun.

CHAPTER NINE

Joseph stood with a breaking heart and watched Mary walk out of his life. The situation was irredeemable and it was a man without hope of consolation who eventually turned back into his home in a bemused and stunned state of mind. Within the space of a few minutes he had been dragged from the mountain streams of blissful love and plunged into the deepest valley of despair. He could find no peace of mind. He paced the floor late into the night and when he finally laid his head down to rest he sobbed himself to sleep. He loved this woman more than words could ever describe, but she had made it impossible for there ever to be a future for them as man and wife. He could not and would not believe her absurd story that her pregnancy was some kind of miracle. Although he was repulsed by the thought, and did find it difficult to believe that his sweet and seemingly pure Mary was capable of it, she had obviously slept with another man and was inventing, in her fear, this wild story of angels and divine visitations as a cover for her guilt. He woke several times from a fitful sleep, wondering if it was all some dreadful nightmare, but each time consciousness confirmed the truth and poured more fuel onto the fires of wretchedness.

The following morning a red-eyed carpenter attempted to carry on his work, first tending to the needs of his children before leaving to repair a client's roof a short distance away. It was very late in the afternoon, as dusk was settling into the lap of the hills, that Joseph heard from one of Mary's neighbours that she was not at home and had not been seen all day. Evidently a local shepherd reported that he saw a young woman of Mary's description very early in the morning walking on the outskirts of the town heading in the direction of Jezreel. She was carrying a bag and he assumed that she was on her way to the city. He remembered thinking that it was a little strange to see such a young woman out by herself at such an early hour, but he had not had the presence of mind to mention it before. Joseph was paralyzed with anxiety. His throat constricted with panic and a wave of nausea sent him weak at the knees. Thoughts too horrible to contemplate raced uncontrollably through his mind as he hastened in a blur of apprehension towards Mary's home in the vain hope that it was all a mistake and that he would find her busy with some household chore. It was evidently not so, for the house was obviously empty. He slumped into a sitting position in the dust with his back against the door and waited until darkness fell. Where could she be? He knew of no one to whom she could go for help. Her parents were both tragically deceased and her only relative that he was aware of was her elder sister who lived in Bethsaida by the lake. It was possible that she had gone there, but he thought it unlikely that she would want to trouble her and her husband with her problems, and anyway, the geography was wrong. The shepherd reported her walking in a southerly direction and Bethsaida was northeast of Nazareth. He was tormented with the thought of her being out there alone in the darkness of the night, defenceless and perhaps suicidal, in danger from the ruthless brigands who preyed on unsuspecting travellers from their hideouts in the hills. He pulled at his beard until it pained him. He wanted to do something, anything, to help, but he knew that he was powerless. He went home, dejected, to his children.

A sleepless night gave way to a difficult day. He was plagued with troublesome questions from his children who loved Mary dearly. They had no intention of quitting their quest for an answer concerning her whereabouts and there were scenes of tearful outbursts, particularly from the younger ones. Joseph's friends regarded him with suspicion. They were understandably perplexed that he offered no explanation for his fiancé's sudden departure and he was too righteous to offer a lie and too honourable to tell them the truth. He simply shrugged his shoulders and opened his arms in a gesture of hopelessness.

Days and nights flowed into one huge whirlpool of worry and frustration, but no news was forthcoming. The Sabbath dawned and he made his way to the Synagogue hoping for a spiritual answer for his valley of gloom. He did in fact receive a glimmer of hope. A faithful old priest by the name of Eliakim told him that Mary once spoke to him of a cousin of hers who was married to a priest who lived not far from Jerusalem. The old man comfortingly squeezed Joseph's arm, smiled reassuringly and suggested that perhaps she had gone there. He was right, of course, but Joseph had no way of discovering whether he was or not. Whatever, it was a possibility, and in that he found a semblance of optimism.

Passing weeks brought with them a mood of resignation. Extreme lassitude took its toll and Joseph felt that he could no longer cope with the uncertainty and worry. Although his love for Mary did not diminish it appeared obvious that she was not intending to return to Nazareth. She was gone forever. She would have her baby somewhere else to avoid the shame which she would inevitably suffer at home and make a life for herself and child in some unknown location. Perhaps she would eventually find solace in the arms of another man. He tried to convince himself that she never really loved him, that she was an impressionable young girl who became infatuated with thoughts of romance and marriage. It was time for him to move on and consider his own future and the security of his suffering children. He was in a peculiar position because he was still legally bound by his espousal to Mary. He had absolutely no desire to publically shame her or place her in danger before the law, but he did now need to be free of it all. He wondered if her prolonged absence might be sufficient grounds for a legal ending of the contract. If so it would free him of his obligations without compromising Mary on moral grounds. Three months had passed since her disappearance and it did not seem reasonable that he should be expected to wait any longer. After much deliberation and heart-searching he finally resolved that on the morrow he would ask the advice of the Rabbi and have him draw up the necessary documents.

He took to his bed in a spirit of regretful purpose. Although it pained him greatly he had at least come to a decision which now brought him, for the moment, a modicum of peace. What he could not do, however, was to extricate himself from the uncanny power of love, and several times throughout the night he woke from sleep wondering where she was and if she was still alive. Perhaps she was torn apart by guilt. He was not sure which experience was the worse, the burden of being betrayed, which he felt was his position, or the burden of living with being the betrayer. Perhaps her suffering was worse than his. He prayed for her safety, and for her peace of mind. Tomorrow he would sever himself from her forever and trust that then he would feel free. His mind was made up but his heart still searched for her. He felt like he was about to sever himself from his own breath. Exhaustion finally conquered his senses and he fell into a deep sleep.

He dreamed that he was spinning in a swirl of feather light clouds, free of the burden of gravity and soaring like an eagle into the blue expanse of heaven, the green earth slipping away beneath him. It was as though he was transported into another world, a place of soothing light cascading down purple mountains and forming pools of crystal water in fertile valleys opulent with verdure. He was flying over rolling hills and flower-strewn meadows, and he could hear music, music such as he had never heard before, and it was the fuel to his flight, the energy which propelled him into paradise. Then he was in a lofty chamber with walls of precious stones and a domed roof of transparent gold. Rays of light poured through the golden glass and divided into the colours of the rainbow, and standing in the centre of the refracted light was the angel of the Lord. Joseph covered his eyes to shield them from the burning light and fell prostrate before the eternal creature. He was shaking with fear. He believed that he was present at the final judgement and he felt so unworthy to stand in this pure and awesome place. The angel spoke with a voice like the roaring of a mighty ocean, yet his words were clear and

easy to understand, echoing around the heavenly atrium and searing like an arrow into the heart of the carpenter.
"Joseph, thou son of David, fear not to take unto thee Mary thy wife, for that which is conceived in her is of the Holy Ghost. And she shall bring forth a Son, and thou shalt call His name Jesus: for He shall save His people from their sins."
Then a voice like the wind of the Spirit of the Almighty was echoing through the air about him and quoting from the book of Isaiah the prophet,
"Behold, a virgin shall be with child, and shall bring forth a Son, and they shall call His name Emmanuel, which being interpreted is, God with us."

Then he was falling, hurtling in free fall through the blackness of night, terror taking his breath as the ground rose to meet him. He was plunging to certain death and he cried to Elohim for help and mercy. Miraculously the wind suddenly swept beneath him and became a cushion to his feet. It caught him, as an eagle catches her fledglings on her wings, and gently lowered him to the earth. He opened his eyes. He was lying in the corner of his room, the faint glow of a new day marking the perimeter of the shutters. He was wet with the sweat of fear and cold with the chill of the morning. He covered his nakedness with a blanket and opened the shutter to gaze with bewilderment into the deserted street. The children were still sleeping. He was physically shaking in the aftermath of the dream as he dressed and slipped quietly out into the crisp, spring morning and made his way up the hill where he and Mary had so often walked together. He breathed deeply, filling his lungs with the fresh exhilarating air, seeking to discern between the reality of consciousness and the validity or otherwise of his unconscious journeying. Could it be true? Was his dream more than just a dream? Was it possible that Mary really was with child of the Holy Ghost? Could it possibly be that his little Mary was the virgin maiden spoken of by the prophet Isaiah hundreds of years before? If so he had seriously misjudged her, condemned an innocent girl and accused her of a sin which she did not commit. She had not lied to him. There was no secret lover. She was the one chosen by God to bear the Messiah. A wave of nausea swept from his depths and engulfed his whole body, rendering him weak at the knees. He sat down heavily on the dew-coated sod as the light of early morning gently washed the flat roofed houses beneath him and, head in hands, sobbed his acceptance of truth. He had unjustly driven away the woman he loved and she would never return. Remorse shuddered through his heart. He had failed not only her, but God, the One who had offered him the opportunity of being a father to His Son. Then, in an instant, hope revived. If she was never going to return why did the angel tell him not to fear to take her as his wife? God knew exactly where she was and if it was His purpose for them to marry He would send her home to him. He climbed uncertainly to his feet, still trembling slightly but with a new expectation dawning in his spirit. Below him Nazareth was stirring from her sleep as the first weak rays of the sun gave notice to the loose pockets of mist which drifted in and out of the grassy hollows that it was time to leave. He lifted his head and his voice in a simple cry to the Lord he loved,

"Please, Oh God of Abraham, send her home to me!"

Feeling considerably calmer he made his way home to wake the children and prepare his work for the day. He fetched fresh water and gave the children breakfast before hurrying them out to their lessons. All thoughts of divorce, and priests, and legal papers, were gone from his mind. He prepared his tool bag and bent to fasten his boots. He still felt weak from the trauma produced by the dream and he felt dizzy as he once more stood erect. He turned and walked slowly towards the door, but as he did so, it was opened by the hand of another. And then she was standing there, silhouetted against the morning light. She looked very nervous, hesitating to intrude if her presence was not welcome. She smiled pensively, like a swimmer tentatively testing the temperature of the water. She looked a little heavier, somewhat fuller in the face, and was glowing with that mysterious beauty which accompanies pregnant women. They each stood silently waiting for the other to speak, but when she ventured to do so he stepped forward and placed his finger gently to her lips, forbidding words. Then he took her gently into his arms as though he believed that she would disintegrate if he held her with the passion which pounded within his chest. He held the softness of her cheek against his own and whispered in her ear.
"I know Mary, I know everything."
The words were like soothing music to her tortured heart and her freely flowing tears soaked his shirt. Tears of his own ran through his beard and into her hair. They held each other close and bathed in the comfort of each other's love.
"I have missed you so much Mary. I have prayed for you every day. I am so sorry. I love you."

He continued to hold her close as he told her how the angel of the Lord had told him the identity of the child she bore and that he should not be afraid to take her to be his wife. He began to plead for her forgiveness, but now her finger touched his mouth requiring silence.

"There is no need for forgiveness Joseph, for you could not possibly have known unless our Lord informed you."

She tenderly drew his face towards her own and softly kissed his repentant lips.

Then they were laughing together, only escaping from each other's arms for time enough to link their souls through the communion of their eyes. Then they were plunging back into the closeness of their fond embrace, excitedly declaring their pledges of mutual love. They laughed and cried with unrestrained joy. They danced across the sawdust of the workshop, finally sitting on the floor together behind an unfinished cabinet, holding hands as though this moment must be made to last forever. He gazed with longing into the windows of her heart and with a voice choking with emotion he said,

"Marry me Mary, now, today, please be my wife."

He was so serious and so romantic in his appeal that he was taken aback by her reaction. She laughed mischievously and tossed the locks of her raven hair across her right shoulder. With her head tilted seductively and her eyes glowing with happiness she replied,

"I suppose I will marry you Joseph. If the angel said I must, then I must!"

So it was that on that very day of her return from Bet Hakerem, the day after the night of Joseph's dream, as the

April sunshine heralded the advent of summer in Israel, the happy couple of destiny were joined in holy matrimony in the presence of their friends and neighbours, and to the absolute delight of Joseph's radiant children.

There was, of course, no sexual union between them until after the birth of Mary's baby.

CHAPTER TEN

Mary and Joseph were very much in love. Their hearts were utterly united, their spirits intertwined in eternal embrace. They swam into each other's eyes and drank the life breath of purest love. They found contentment in unspoken mutual adoration. Yet for them the unbridled passion which expresses the overwhelming love of newly married couples was not expedient. Their bodies yearned to become one in an expression of the union of their souls and they found it difficult to share a bed without consummating their marriage, but it must not be. There were no legal reasons why they should not become physically one because all the constraints of the moral law were now lifted, but somehow they both instinctively knew that to engage in sexual union before the birth of the Christ was unacceptable. It was essential that no possible question could be raised in future times relative to the identity of the father of Mary's child. The salvation of human kind depended upon the divinity of the Saviour and no fuel must be offered to the fires of scepticism that would certainly be lit across the span of history. They both needed to be able to truthfully declare that there was no sexual union between them until after the birth of Jesus. So the happy couple lay contentedly in each other's arms, sometimes nose to nose, lips to lips, thankful for their shared love and understanding, and talked baby talk until they fell asleep. Mary discovered in these nightly discourses that her beloved carpenter had actually delivered his wife's first child Justus and had been present at the births of all his children. His experience was to prove useful.

The weeks following the marriage were a period of blissful happiness in the home of Joseph, son of Jacob. The children were ecstatic, savouring every moment of attention from their new mother. The carpentry rang with laughter and Mary was the happiest that she could ever remember. After much thought and consideration the happy couple decided to wait for a few weeks before sharing the news of their expected addition with the children, although Mary's waistline was now rapidly disappearing and changes in her body were becoming more noticeable. It would not be long before people would make their observations, do their calculations, and form their judgements. A sense of apprehension began to invade the boundaries of her joy.

The first indication of the impending storm arrived on a bright, sunny morning as Mary was buying fruit in the town's small market place. She noticed a woman who was familiar to her (she remembered sitting next to her in the Synagogue) gazing intently at her slightly swollen belly. The woman turned and spoke to her companion whilst at the same time inclining her head in Mary's direction. The second woman looked across and made her own inspection. Mary looked away. She had no idea what to do. It was soon going to become impossible to conceal the fact that she was with child, or the fact that she must have been pregnant before she married Joseph. People were not fools. She reasoned that if Joseph had refused to believe her story then there was absolutely no way that the general public could be expected to accept it, even if she was prepared to tell them the truth. Horrendous problems lay ahead which were destined to make herself and Joseph, and their children, outcasts in their own community. She made herself turn again in the direction of the still staring gossips, smiled sweetly to them, and made her way home.

That night the candles burned low in their room as she told Joseph about the incident in the market square. She expressed her fears, especially for the children and it seemed that wisdom required that they speak with them first thing the following morning and explain to them that their mother was going to have a baby. They decided to tell them that they were free to share the news with all their friends and whoever else they wished to tell. They also agreed that they would now speak openly to their neighbours, customers and friends, and share their joy with all and sundry. They concluded that if any of these chose to murmur or be judgemental there was absolutely nothing they could do, or should try and do, to prevent it. They determined to maintain a buoyant and happy spirit whatever the future threw at them. Nothing must be allowed to take away their joy. They held hands in the half-light and committed their circumstances to Elohim. Joseph blew out the candle and they fell asleep wrapped in each other's arms.

Mary was much relieved when several weeks passed with no sign of hostility or rejection. She knew that it would not last, but was determined to enjoy the present calm before the storm broke. Her peace was finally shattered when one afternoon the children came home crying. Esther was sobbing uncontrollably as she burst into the house and ran distraught into Mary's arms.
"Mummy, my friend Deborah said that her mother and father don't want her to play with me any more."

"It's because of the baby," said Justus. "Everyone is saying that you were having the baby before you were married." He turned to face Joseph. "Is that true father?"

"Sit down here all of you."
Joseph held out his hand and motioned to his children to be seated on the mats which were arranged neatly across the concrete floor. Justus defiantly remained standing, determined to have an answer to his question before he would obey.
"Is it true father?" he repeated with more than a hint of insolence.
Joseph's response was equally firm.
"Sit down Justus, and show some respect."
The boy reluctantly complied and Joseph sat down with them, cross-legged on the floor. Mary quietly, sedately, knelt at her husband's side. Joseph spoke softly but with an unmistakable authority his children had never felt from him before.
"The scripture tells us that one day God will send the Messiah as the Saviour of the Jewish people. He will be born in the line of the great King David. The prophet tells us that he will be born of a young woman who has never been with a man. Now before Mary went away,"- he paused to ask the question, "You remember that she went away for three months?" They nodded. They remembered- "Well, before she went away she came and told me that an angel had appeared to her and told her that she was chosen by God to be the young woman who would be the mother of the Messiah. I did not believe her and that is why she left so suddenly. The night before she arrived home God took me in a dream into the presence of an angel who informed

me that what Mary told me before she went away was true and that I should take her to be my wife. So you see Justus, Mary was with child before our marriage, but neither of us did anything wrong. The people who criticise us do not understand and unfortunately they would not believe us if we tried to explain. I do not blame them for their anger but I do not expect you to be angry. I expect you to believe that we are telling you the truth because we love you and would never tell you a lie."

The younger ones certainly failed to grasp the meaning of their father's words, but they all felt the sweet liberating atmosphere of truth, and peace drove away the tension from the room. Judas was the first to break the silence.

"So will the new baby be our brother?"

Joseph smiled. "Of course he will be your brother Judas. God has asked me to be His father, so my children must be His brothers and sisters."

Esther took hold of Mary's hand. "So will your baby live in a palace, mummy?"

"Of course not little one," Mary replied. "He will live here with us."

Justus said nothing but the anger had gone from his eyes. Joseph thought how like his mother he was. He certainly had her forthright manner and fiery spirit. The boy stood up to leave the room, but paused to lay a reassuring hand upon his new mother's shoulder. He caught his father's eye and the hint of a smile edged the corners of his mouth.

The young couple lay awake for a long time that night and speculated about the immediate future. They both knew that dark storm clouds were gathering over their small but well- known home. There was not a person in Nazareth who did not know Joseph the carpenter and his sudden marriage to Mary following her prolonged absence had been the talk of the town. Now Joseph and Mary were to become the object of unrestrained scorn and ridicule. They would be despised by the entire populace and their children would be ostracised and persecuted.

"We must pray for them every day Joseph, that God will protect them and help them to believe the truth when everyone is telling them lies about us. We must pray that God will use the difficult days ahead to make them strong in character for the future."

They prayed together for a while until Joseph's heavy breathing told her that his weary body had succumbed to sleep. She prayed that God would give him strength to bear the many burdens of misunderstanding and persecution that he was destined to shoulder. A solitary tear ran down her face as she held the strong arm of the man God had given her. Though so close to her sleeping husband she suddenly felt very alone and a feeling of trepidation drifted like a cold, clammy cloud across her spirit. Then deep inside the darkness of her body she felt an unmistakable flutter as for the first time she felt the movement of the unborn Christ within her womb. It was as though the Almighty God was whispering a secret to his special handmaiden, assuring her that all was well. She laid both her hands on the place where she had felt Him kick and hoped for a replay of the action. Though none was forthcoming she fell asleep with a smile of contentment upon her lips.

CHAPTER ELEVEN

Mary showed outstanding courage and resolve through the remaining months of her pregnancy. She held her head high and maintained her dignity in the face of extreme adversity. Rumours incubated overnight and infiltrated the homes of the people of Nazareth like a contagious disease. The most common assumption was that Joseph and Mary had indulged in premarital sex and then married quickly in an attempt to cover up the truth. Others, however, remembered Mary's unexpected and unexplained departure from home and her subsequent three months of absence. Using the evidence of Joseph's unquestionably unfeigned anguish and anxiety during that time they concluded that she had been unfaithful to her espoused and was pregnant by a third party. One rumour had it that Mary formed a liaison with a Roman soldier who was the father of her unborn child. In later years this dreadful fabrication was embellished by actually naming the military paramour, said to be a Roman by the name of Panthern. However understandable the bewilderment of the people of Nazareth may be, there is no doubt that they overstepped the parameters of fair-mindedness and degenerated into a state of excessive and offensive murmuring.

The town gossip inevitably had a detrimental effect on Joseph's business. Even those who were not themselves malicious were reluctant to employ the carpenter for fear of recriminations from those who were. The general poverty with which Joseph's family were already acquainted became more extreme and, although he certainly gave himself energetically to whatever work he could find, he grew weaker for lack of food. He unbendingly insisted that Mary and the children should have what little food they could afford to buy. He prayed much, and they prayed together, and on more than one occasion when it seemed as though they would not survive, bags of provisions mysteriously appeared at the carpentry door, evidence that God had troubled the conscience of some unidentified neighbour.

The humiliation of Mary was extreme. She was regarded as nothing better than a whore, ostracised by the whole community, and nobody would openly communicate or speak with her. Individuals openly spat into the dust as she passed by and the gasp of horror which rose from the congregation of the Synagogue when she dared to attend Sabbath services was heartfelt and deliberate. She found herself sitting by herself with empty seats all around her, making her an open target for the hateful looks of contempt that were fired at her from every side. Abusive words were shouted at her in the streets and graffiti calling for her death by stoning marred the walls of her home. Notwithstanding these manifold trials and tribulations the happiness of the family could not be quenched. The joy and laughter and excitement that radiated from their lives was evidence enough that those who walk in the purity of truth need not be intimidated by the hostility of those who do not. Mutual respect bound Joseph and Mary together like chains of iron. Their love and loyalty to each other acted as an invisible force which stood like an unmoveable rock against the fury of the storm. Their example also fortified their children against the undeserved abuse which they inevitably received.

Mary's love for her unborn son grew with every passing day. She lived with an unfailing sense of awe that, growing within her womb was a human being fathered by Almighty God. The aura of unreality was disproved by the fact and the immensity of her love was paralleled only by her wonderment. She gave much time to the study of the scriptures to discover as much information relative to the Messiah as she could. Her exploration uncovered conflicting and confusing conclusions. On the one hand she found prophesies predicting that the Messiah would be a great deliverer destined for exaltation and glory, a future king of Israel greater than his forefather David. His kingdom would be a kingdom of peace, a rule that would know no end. On the other hand there were prophecies relating to the Messiah which promised rejection and pain, suffering, agony, and gruesome, bloody death. No matter how hard she tried she found it impossible to reconcile the apparent contradictions. Her powerful motherly instincts wanted to embrace the promise of future glory for her son, ignore or explain away the negative, and believe for the best, but deep within her heart she experienced a sense of powerful foreboding, like an ocean of pain gathering inside her soul and waiting to burst and drown her in a torrent of grief. Sometimes the emotion was so overwhelming that she wanted to wail with premature heartbreak. Periodically she discerned the proximity of the foul beast which she saw on the night of her conception and she wanted to scream it away into the darkness. She received little or no help with her mental and spiritual torments from

Joseph. Her well-meaning husband was only interested in comforting his wife by assuring her that she was being unnecessarily pessimistic and that everything in the future would be wonderful. He refused to even consider what he regarded to be a negative view of the scriptures and insisted on pointing out that the Rabbis taught that the Messiah would be the greatest king that Israel had ever known, and were not they the experts in the exegesis of scripture? After several bouts of prolonged worry about an unknown and distant future Mary committed it all into the will of the Lord and decided to live one day at a time. Her peace was thereby restored and laughter once more filled her soul.

God's chosen virgin refused to allow the hatred and hostility of her neighbours to imprison her in her home, insisting on taking walks each evening with her husband for both exercise and relaxation. At first she braved the summer heat and climbed the hills, but as she grew heavy with child she restricted her activity to walks through the vineyards and olive groves to the huge palm tree beyond. There they sat under the shade afforded by the ample leaves and enjoyed each other in the cool of the evening, talking about everything and nothing. They returned to the carpentry ruddy from the fresh air and the late afternoon sun and with their arms ladened with small posies of wild flowers plucked from the grassy banks. The blooms adorned their rooms for a number of hours before wilting and expiring, to be replaced by fresh flowers the following evening. Occasionally their excursions were sullied by the verbal abuse which was hurled at them by ignorant passers-by, but the insults were suitably ignored and died into insignificance.

Mid-September induced cooler breezes thereby making life a little more bearable for the pregnant teenager who was now only a matter of weeks away from giving birth. Then came the news that they were required to embark upon a seven or eight day journey southward, beyond Jerusalem, to a little town called Bethlehem in Judea, in order to register their names in a national census. The idea was preposterous. Mary was in no fit condition to make such a journey. An attempt to travel on the back of an ass over hostile terrain when about to deliver a baby, with five young children to care for, one of them only three years of age, was completely unthinkable. It struck fear into Mary's heart.
"But Joseph," she wept, "I cannot do it. What if my baby is born when we are out on the road? He might die. I will not do it. I will not put my baby's life at risk. It is my duty to protect him even if in doing so I defy the edict of Rome."

That night she lay, too troubled to sleep, picturing the long and arduous journey to Bethlehem. She was determined not to go; yet she was afraid of the consequences of such disobedience. Joseph slept soundly at her side and the stillness of the night did nothing to alleviate her apprehension. She mentally scanned the scriptures which referred to the Messiah for she knew that she must at all times trust the Architect of her circumstances to care both for her and her baby. A faint memory struggled to the surface of her mind, a recollection that somewhere in her reading she had seen some obscure reference to the town of Bethlehem. She slipped out of bed and, having kindled the lamp, opened her much loved book. She searched for more than an hour before eventually finding the place. It was in the book of the prophet Micah and as she read her heart was lifted. She whispered the words into the darkness and allowed the revelation they brought to wash away her fears.

"But thou, Bethlehem Ephratah, though thou be little among the thousands of Judah, yet out of thee shall He come forth unto Me that is to be the ruler in Israel: whose goings forth have been from of old, from everlasting."

She sat stunned with wonderment. It was her answer. The summons to Bethlehem was no accident. It was the purpose of God from the beginning of time that His Son should be born there. By ordering the census the power of Rome was an unwitting tool in the hand of the Almighty to fulfil His purpose for the birthplace of His Son.

Mary was moving about before dawn busily bundling together necessities for their journey. She packed as much food as she could and plenty of water. Then she woke Joseph and the children and read to them the passage in the book of Micah which had changed her mind. She was ready to set out for Bethlehem. Joseph responded positively to the unexpected turn of events and smiled proudly at his wife as she gave her instructions to the family. Justus would hold Esther's hand, Simon and Judas would stay together, and little Tamar would ride on her father's shoulders or sit with Mary on the back of their faithful old donkey who was affectionately known to all of them as Dan. The children leaped around with excitement in anticipation of the adventure of such a journey and their squeals of delight floated out into the street. Joseph checked that they had everything they needed and to the uncontrollable sound of turbulent chatter the little group of travellers headed out of town, through the pretty gorge strewn with the wild flowers of early autumn, and down through the valley towards Jezreel. Joseph's troubled eyes repeatedly roamed anxiously across the bursting belly of his wife as she swayed back and forth in tandem with the gait of the ass. He prayed that she would make it to their destination.

CHAPTER TWELVE

The Roman Emperor, Caesar Augustus, made registers of his empire and its tributary states, partly to bolster his own prestige, but mainly for taxation purposes. This procedure, of course, included the state of Palestine. The Roman method of documentation required populations to register their individual names in the city nearest to their place of birth. The Jewish procedure of census was traditionally done more by tribe than actual place of birth, although for many Israelis their tribal ancestry was unknown. For Jews living at the time when Cyrenius was governor of Syria the system of registration was a mixture of the two and required either a journey to one's place of birth or to a city representing one's tribal origins. In the case of Joseph and Mary the Roman way would have been more convenient as they both still lived in their home town, but because their tribal ancestries were both known to be in the lineage of David, whose city was Bethlehem, and Herod, for political reasons, favoured the Jewish system wherever possible, it was incumbent upon them to make the journey to Judea.

Joseph considered it prudent to avoid the hostile regions of Samaria and decided on the route that would take them east to the Jordan Valley. They would then follow the river southwards as far as the fords of Jericho and then southwest through the Judean wilderness to their final destination. It would take them at least a week and he knew that it would be a very difficult journey, especially with such young children and a pregnant wife. He did his utmost to introduce high spirits from the outset, pointing out interesting landmarks and playing "Spot the Wildlife" with his children. It was, however, a massive challenge and the younger ones were understandably completely exhausted before the first nightfall. Their camping equipment was of the crudest kind and they spent a very uncomfortable night in the shelter of a huge rock. Fortunately the weather was good and Joseph knew that it would still be quite hot in the river valley. He did not expect any rain because the first rains did not usually begin until the middle of October.

The second day did not get off to a good start. Aches and pains from the previous day's journey joined forces with blistered feet and numerous insect bites to produce tears and constant requests for rest. Tamar wanted to go home. Justus quite innocently asked his father if there were any snakes in the long grass and immediately spread panic and fear amongst his brothers and sisters. Mary insisted on taking her turn to walk in order to give the children opportunity to ride the donkey, but she was now within just a few days of giving birth and her progress on foot was painfully slow. On day three they reached the river. The valley was magnificent. The worst of the summer heat, which had risen to unbearable temperatures during the last three months, was now past and although it was still very warm it was not unpleasant. They ate their fill of fruit from the wild fig trees, and pomegranates, yellow dates and bananas grew in abundance and were ripe for harvest. The full branches of the tropical date palms provided much needed shelter from the midday sun and the numerous fresh water springs were a source of replenishment for their depleted water bags. Joseph demonstrated such patient care for his pregnant wife, such understanding of the needs of the little ones, such selfless devotion to duty, and above all, such a buoyant attitude, that Mary marvelled at his goodness and strength. Each day the children seemed to grow stronger as they adjusted to the nomadic life, but each day she grew weaker and more apprehensive. She knew that her baby could come at any time and she prayed constantly as the ass jolted and pitched across the uncertain terrain.

It took seven days to traverse the fifty-five miles of the Jordan Valley and arrive at the fords of Jericho. From here the real trial began in the form of the torturous uphill journey through the Judean wilderness to Bethlehem. Jericho marked the end of the valley of plenty and the beginning of the desert of pain. No more level ground to walk, just barren hills and rugged peaks to ascend and descend with repetitive agony. They had to carry enough food and water to see them through at least another three days of travel, most of it up hill. From 400 metres below sea level, the lowest point on earth, to 800 metres above sea level, they must climb through the most hostile territory imaginable. It seemed an impossible task to the pregnant woman, but she bravely struggled on, constantly reminding herself of Micah's prophecy designating Bethlehem as the birthplace of the Messiah. Joseph appeared bright and confident, but secretly he was plagued with doubt and feared that they would not make it. Justus, who was old enough to understand something of the awesome task before them, wept as he walked. The temperature cooled as they climbed but the children cried with pain from blistered feet and aching limbs. Mary could no longer walk so she tried to carry the children with her on the back of the ass, but there was so little room and her discomfort was extreme. Joseph tried to help by carrying them one at a time on his shoulders, but he was now wilting under the load and the pain in his aching back became intolerable. He was torn between the need for regular rest periods and the urgent need for his wife to reach Bethlehem. They slept under the Judean stars and Joseph prayed earnestly to the God of Israel for the survival of his family.

It was noon on the fourteenth day of travel when they had their first sight of the distant Bethlehem. She stood clearly visible on the lofty hillside, a proud challenge to the exhausted travellers to make the final climb. Mary said nothing to Joseph but the flood of water that announced the imminent birth of her son had already spilled from her womb across the back of the donkey and the first pangs of labour were tightening around her midriff. Every clumsy step of the faithful old animal sent tearing pain through her abdomen as she tried to calculate the distance still left to travel. The impressive view of the castle above them deceptively promised an imminent end to her hellish journey, but, no matter how hard they drove on, it seemed to hold them at a distance. She cried out with the pains of labour as they pushed on through the fruitful vineyards that littered the ascent. The light was receding and the cool bite of the autumnal evening closed in before they finally reached the outskirts of the town. There were people everywhere. The census had succeeded in doubling the population of Bethlehem and the streets were teeming with visitors enjoying the evening together. Mary, finding it difficult to cope with the searing contractions which were now stealing her breath every few minutes, tried in vain to stifle the cries of pain which burst involuntarily from her broken lips. She slid from the donkey's back and attempted to walk, but her feet and ankles were swollen with fluid and the pain was doubling her over. Passers by stared with incredulity at the woman who was obviously about to bring forth a child in the open street. From house to house and inn to inn her anxious husband sought shelter for his wife and children, but there was no room available. Tamar was crying uncontrollably and Mary was now audibly calling on God for help and mercy.

"Save me, O God; for the waters are come in unto my soul. I sink in deep mire, where there is no standing: I am come into deep waters, where the floods overflow me. I am weary of my crying: my throat is dried: mine eyes fail while I wait for my God. For Thy sake I have borne reproach; shame hath covered my face. They that sit in the gate speak against me; and I was the song of the drunkards. But as for me, my prayer is unto Thee, O Lord: O God, in the multitude of Thy mercy hear me. Deliver me out of the mire, and let me not sink. Let not the water flood overflow me, neither let the deep swallow me up, and let not the pit shut her mouth upon me."

As Joseph banged frantically on the door of yet another inn his wife reached the end of her endurance and could fight no more. She surrendered to the cold ground and wrapped her arms protectively around her unborn babe as another seizure of unbearable pain ripped through her inside.

The innkeeper was a kindly man and looked sympathetically across at the suffering young woman who was lying in the street propped up by her weeping children. Joseph explained his wife's predicament and pleaded with the man for help. After a short and frenzied exchange he ran to Mary's side.

"He says we can make ourselves beds in the animal area. It's better than nothing Mary; at least you will be able to lie down there. I will make you a bed with some straw. I will look after you."

She smiled weakly, but sadly.

"My dear husband, am I to give birth to the Messiah in a stall with the beasts of the field?"

The stench of the animals was nauseating. The atmosphere was filled with dust from the straw and the odour from the urine-soaked floor polluted the air. The temperature was chilled to say the least. Mary was right. This was no place for any baby to be born, let alone for the future King of Israel, the Son of the Most High God. She slumped into a corner and wept with despair and fear. She never knew pain like this before. It was as though a band of steel was wrapped around her middle and was being intermittently tightened like a huge tourniquet. She found it difficult to breathe, as though a huge weight was pressed against her chest, crushing the life out of her body. Her bones ached from the long journey and her mind was tormented with thoughts of demons and death. A dreadful terror that her baby would die in the struggle for birth suddenly drained the air from her lungs and she released a pitiful cry of anguish.

He made her a mattress of straw and covered it with his coat. He found a piece of wood to use as a makeshift pillow and gently carried his beloved Mary to her bed of labour.

He confined the animals to an area behind a wall of hay and pieces of timber and made separate compartments between bales of straw for the children to rest. He comforted each of them as he lay them down and, utterly exhausted, they fell instantly to sleep. Then he cleaned out the drinking trough of the animals and lined it with fresh straw and covered it carefully with material torn from his shirt. As darkness fell he lit the lamp that was hanging from a nail in the rafters and sat down and held her hand. All was ready for the birth of Emmanuel.

He winced with every agonising cry that forced its way passed her unyielding lips. He felt nervous, not because he doubted his ability to attend the birth, but because of the strange atmosphere which filled this lowly place. He could sense the unseen, as though in some intangible realm, forces of light were contending with forces of darkness for supremacy in an event vital to the history of human kind. He felt alone, but also knew that this matter was being watched by powers he could not see. Mary was crying out every minute now. She gripped his arm and arched her back in the throes of her agony. She tore at her clothes in the delirium of pain and her naked belly contorted in the struggle as her child fought to survive. Joseph resorted to weeping as she grew weary in the fight to bring him forth. He whispered his love into her ear in the short intervals between the pangs, but extreme fatigue, a lassitude of body and mind, was robbing her of her will to go on. She was now lapsing into periods of unconsciousness and he feared that she would be lost to him forever.
"Joseph," she gasped. "I can't do it any more. I am so sorry but I have no more strength."

It was as though heaven held its breath. Another shuddering contraction tore her open. Then her eyes opened in stark terror and a look of horror drained the colour from her swollen face. She held onto Joseph's arm as though she feared she would slide into some dark abyss.

"Joseph!" she panted. "Help me, Joseph! The dragon is here!"

She could see it, its ugly fiendish jaws spread yawning wide before her open legs, waiting to devour her baby at the moment of His birth. Its eyes were huge, bloodshot and hungry, its knurled teeth black and obscene. In that moment it seemed that she would die, but the vision of the dragon drew from her the final fading vestige of her strength. With her last remaining energy she cursed the dragon in the name of Elohim and at the same time exerted herself in one last push. The dragon fled before the all-powerful Name and she felt the infant slide from within her into the tender hands of Joseph. She listened in what seemed to be an eternal silence for the cry that would tell her that all was well. Then she was holding Him in her arms and nestling His bloodied face against her naked breast.

She tore a piece of cloth from her undergarment and used it as a shawl. She wrapped Him carefully within its folds and Joseph placed the priceless bundle into the unique cradle which he had prepared. Mary lay back upon her bloodstained bed of straw and breathed relief and spent emotion into the night air. The stable swayed slightly as she yielded to unconsciousness.

Two hours later she was awakened by people moving about around her bed. She instinctively looked to the protection of her baby and saw Joseph standing at the manger cradle with a group of men she had never seen before. They were peering at her baby and muttering excitedly to each other. She was understandably afraid that something was wrong. Who were these strange men who invaded her privacy in the middle of the night? One of the men realised that Mary was awake and immediately offered his apologies for intruding at such an unacceptable hour, but explained that they were a group of shepherds who were tending their sheep on the hill just outside of the town when angels appeared in the skies to announce the birth of the Saviour, the Messiah. They had hurried into town that they might see the infant Christ and that they might worship Him. Mary smiled weakly as, one by one, the ruddy-faced shepherds knelt before her baby son and gazed with awe into the face of the infant Redeemer. After several minutes Joseph gently suggested that his wife was very tired and needed to rest and the grateful men graciously acquiesced and, bowing low to the virgin mother, disappeared into the night. The baby cried and Joseph tenderly lifted Him from the trough and placed Him in the arms of His mother. He searched hungrily for her milk.

"See this Joseph," she whispered. "This little babe I suckle at my breast is the Messiah. His father is God himself. And I, little Mary from Nazareth, am His mother. And this, this poor and dirty animal house, is the birthplace of the King."

Joseph placed his rough hand gently upon the head of his adopted son.

"I thank you, God of Abraham, for this precious gift. I thank you for appointing me to be a husband to Mary and a father to your Son. Please give me wisdom to do what I must do to guard Him and protect Him for the performance of your will."

They all slept until the sun rose and when the children stirred to the sound of disgruntled and complaining animals they had a new baby brother.

Eight days later Mary proudly carried her newborn son into the Synagogue at Bethlehem. She was there for the official naming of her baby, and also for the enacting of the painful rite of circumcision upon Him. According to the Law of Moses every Jewish male had to be circumcised as a symbol of acceptance into the covenant between God and Israel. She placed Him in the arms of the priest and cringed as the divine representative took the knife and inflicted the first pain, the first of many pains, upon her son. Then they named Him according to the instructions given by the angel.

"His name is Jesus," she announced.

The name in Hebrew was 'Joshua' but Mary's child was not named after the great historic deliverer who took Israel into her Promised Land. Neither was He named after the high priest of the same name who led the returning Jewish captives from their exile in Babylon. This Joshua was so named by the instruction of Divinity, not in remembrance of the past, but in prophetic declaration of the work of salvation which He would accomplish for the entire world.

"Thou shalt call His name Jesus, for He shall save His people from their sins."

CHAPTER THIRTEEN

Joseph managed to secure the rental of a semi permanent lodging house in Bethlehem that offered considerably more living space and comfort than the animal house. Employment for someone possessing his expertise with timber was in plentiful supply and he saw no necessity to hasten back to the hostile environment of Nazareth.

When Jesus was forty days old his parents took him to the Temple at Jerusalem. There were a further two requirements of the law with which they must comply, namely Mary's ritual purification after giving birth, and the official presentation of their newborn child to God. The journey from Bethlehem to Jerusalem was a pleasant one. Although Jerusalem is a mountain city Bethlehem stands a little higher in altitude which provided a gentle gradient of approximately six miles for the family to walk. The late November weather was cold, but the sky was blue and the sharp morning air was exhilarating as they set out. They paused at David's Well on the outskirts of the town and Joseph took the time to recount the famous story from long ago. David had been hiding in the cave called Adullam and was at war with the Philistines. In a moment of desperation and nostalgia he one day cried out, "Oh that one would give me a drink of water from the well of Bethlehem which is by the gate!" He didn't really mean it and he certainly never anticipated that anybody would actually go. He was just expressing his feelings of home sickness for his beloved Bethlehem, the place of his birth and the scene of his upbringing. Three of his most

trusted and loyal soldiers, however, heard David's request and risked their lives by fighting their way through enemy lines and brought to him a drink from the well. David was so moved by his friends devotion that he poured out the water as a thank offering to God.
"And this is the very same well," Joseph said. "See, feel the stones."
The children, one by one, touched the memory of ancient dedication and a silent reverence stayed their lips for several minutes as they walked.

About a mile out of Bethlehem they passed the tomb of Rachel, the much loved wife of Jacob. She died a thousand years before whilst giving birth to her second son, Benjamin. Jacob tenderly buried her at the side of the road when on his way to join his father, Isaac, at Mamre. Joseph once again delayed the excursion to explain the moving love story from long ago before they continued their descent. They could see Jerusalem spread magnificently before them like a capital waiting for its king.

They approached the metropolis by skirting the western bank of the valley of Hinnom which was a deep, natural protection to the south and west of the upper city. Rounding the northern edge of the valley they passed the spectacular Palace of Herod on their right and then turned into the city itself through Gennath Gate, heading eastward towards the famous and glorious Temple. Mary was silent as she carried her baby through Coponious Gate, one of four gates on the western wall, and entered the house of God. She was overwhelmed with a feeling of awe and wonderment. This was the very ground where centuries before the great patriarch Abraham tied his son Isaac to the altar in a staggering act of obedience to God and she suddenly felt a mysterious kinship with the man from long ago, like she was somehow walking in his footsteps. She was possessed of a feeling that she was living history in the present and carrying her own baby son to the same dreadful place of sacrifice. An icy chill ran through her flesh. She shivered involuntarily.

Joseph guided his family through the thousands of people who thronged the vast and glorious edifice until they reached the area known as the Court of the Women. Here they could purchase the sacrifice that was necessary for the ceremony of Mary's purification. Normally this consisted of a lamb for a burnt offering and a dove for a sin offering, but for the very poor, who could not afford the cost of these, a pair of turtledoves or two young pigeons would suffice. For the struggling family from Nazareth it was the latter.

The superintending priest watched carefully as Mary deposited her payment for the birds into one of the numerous trumpet shaped chests before making her way respectfully to join the many other women who were there for the same purpose as herself. The resonating tones of the temple orchestra heralded the offering of the incense upon the golden altar and Mary thankfully observed with rapt attention as her sacrifice was offered. The ritual complete she smiled and turned away, Levitical clean. Now she must redeem her first-born son. According to Jewish law every first son in an Israeli family belonged to God and must be ceremonially bought back by the parents. The tradition originated in ancient history when the Jewish people were slaves in the land of Egypt and the first-born sons of Israel were saved from the death that was judgementally inflicted upon the sons of Egypt. The protection was provided by the application of the blood of lambs upon the doorposts and lintels of their homes. From then on the deliverance of Israel from Egypt was remembered at the feast of Passover, when they all feasted on roast lamb, and all the first-born sons in Israel were regarded as belonging to God by right. They could be redeemed, however, for the small sum of five shekels in order that their earthly parents might care for them. It served as a reminder of God's goodness to their nation and of His power to deliver people from slavery of every kind. It was fitting that the son of Mary should be redeemed in this way in order that He might in future days give Himself willingly back to His father to be the Passover Lamb and shed His blood as the redemption price for the whole of mankind. Mary handed her babe into the hands of the priest in acknowledgement of the Divine ownership and, for five shekels, received Him back to love Him and teach Him on behalf of His heavenly Father.

There was at that time a devout and godly Jew living in Jerusalem by the name of Simeon. He was a passionate believer in the coming of the Messiah and he lived a holy life in communion with God. The Holy Spirit had spoken to this old man and told him that before he died he would personally see the Christ. On the same morning that Mary and her family arrived in Jerusalem to present Jesus to the priest, Simeon rose early from his bed with his stomach churning with anticipation. He was overwhelmed with the thought that this was the very special day that he would see the Messiah. He felt drawn, almost compelled, to visit the Temple. He had no idea what to expect, but he made his way to the house of God and pushed his way through the crowds that thronged the Temple Courts. A multitude of questions flooded his mind. How would he recognise Him? How old would He be? How would he know if he met Him? Would He look different from others? It seemed rather an absurd mission, but the more he moved amongst the crowds the more his spirit surged with expectation. The women were there with their babies, for purification and redemption, just as any other day.

He walked for hours amongst the people and his legs were aching and weary before he almost collided with a young girl who was just receiving her baby back from the arms of the priest. He would have passed by, but a sudden quickening in his spirit arrested him as he gazed into the face of the infant and in an instant he knew that he was looking into the eyes of the Son of God. His heart pounded and his throat constricted with emotion as he stood speechless before the One who was the consolation of Israel, the very embodiment of God. How amazing that the Almighty had guided him through the multitudes of people to meet this tiny child. The parents of the baby seemed a little disconcerted at his attention and began to move away, their purpose now completed.

"Excuse me young woman, but may I please hold your baby for a moment?"

His voice was gentle and his eyes were kind, and a perceptive mother hesitated for only a second. She glanced away momentarily to receive Joseph's approval and then carefully cradled her little one in the arms of the old man.

His shining eyes glistened with tears and a voice breaking with emotion began to pray.

"Lord, now lettest thou thy servant depart in peace, according to thy word: for mine eyes have seen thy salvation, which thou hast prepared before the face of all people; a light to lighten the Gentiles, and the glory of thy people Israel."

Mary and Joseph stood in awe of the prophetic words of the stranger and Mary was trembling as the frail old servant of God handed Jesus back into her arms. He smiled into her eyes and spoke again.

"This child is set for the fall and rising again of many in Israel; and for a sign which shall be spoken against."

Then he paused and his eyes exuded love and care as he tenderly held the shoulders of the sweet young girl before him. He could feel some dreadful sorrow, some excruciating agony, waiting for her up ahead, and his soul ached for her grief.

"Yea, a sword shall pierce through thy own soul also."

Mary registered Simeon's words with a wave of recognition. They came as no real surprise for she had felt a witness of future pain in her own spirit many times when reading the gloomy words of scripture relating to the suffering of the Messiah, but it was nevertheless a little disconcerting to hear these powerful and eloquent words from the lips of a stranger. The old man gently squeezed her arms and turned away with tears flowing generously into his grey-white beard. Once more the family from Galilee turned to leave, but now another admirer of their newborn child presented more delay. She was a very old woman, older than Simeon. Her name was Anna, a prophetess, who spent the whole of her time, day and night, in the Temple, praying and seeking God with prayer and fasting. She now presented herself before Mary and began to praise the Lord, accosting and passionately announcing to the people passing by that here was the One who had come to bring redemption to Israel. She was such a happy, buoyant soul, so obviously in communion with God and so uplifting to the spirit of the somewhat bewildered Mary.

Joseph again guided his family through the crowds, no longer noticing the fine architecture, the ornate extravagance, or the many activities going on in the Temple. He and his family had been touched by the unknown, given a glimpse into the wonder of the divine purpose, and yet tasted the unnerving aura of a sorrow yet to be. It was time to head for home. The children were tired and it was a very long walk back to Bethlehem.

That night, as the sun splashed Bethlehem with its dying rays, and its citizens prepared for sleep, Mary prepared herself for her husband. She bathed in their simple wash tub, scenting the water with wild rose petals which she had gathered from the hedgerows in the local hills. She had made her own perfumed skin lotion from olive oil fragranced with the blooms of the Shoshan lily. She massaged it into her skin until her flesh shone in the candlelight, and she brushed her hair until it reflected the flickering flames. It was more than six months since they took their vows before the priest in Nazareth and she had not yet tasted the delights of physical love. The children were asleep, her baby was well-fed and contented, and Joseph was more handsome and desirable than ever.

She stood before him and felt the caress of his eyes as they took in her shapely form. Then she felt the touch of his lips against her own. Their eyes burned with love and passion. For a moment they looked deep into each other's souls and then they were together in the blissful abandonment of mutual love. They rode the shoreline of ecstasy, locked now forever in the total unrestrained union and oneness of their marriage. They felt nothing but love. The whole world seemed to sing a love song. They lay together in naked embrace. They loved God, they loved each other, they loved their children, and they loved their little infant Son of God.

CHAPTER FOURTEEN

A bright-eyed toddler was playing contentedly in the dusty doorway of a small carpentry on the outskirts of Bethlehem. His black curly hair framed his rather chubby cheeks and a mischievous smile edged his lips as he poured a handful of dust into a small earthenware pot in which recent rainwater had accumulated. He proceeded to stir the mixture with both hands until it became a lovely soft-textured mud. He then stood in triumphant disarray and carefully wiped the brown paint over his bare legs.

It was the beginning of May and the infant Jesus was almost nineteen months old. Joseph was out repairing a neighbour's fence not far away and Mary was hanging washing out to dry in the morning sunshine. She was humming contentedly as she worked, casting repeated motherly glances in the direction of her little son. She laughed aloud as he revelled in his earthy concoction. Pleased with her amusement he smiled playfully and deliberately wiped his muddy hands across his cheeks, looking to her for another display of merriment. Her attention, however, was diverted by the noise being made by a group of local people who were mounting the slope leading to her home. They were excitedly accompanying a caravan of camels that were carrying some foreign looking gentlemen. They were dressed lavishly in the colourful garb of wealthy eastern stock and their skin was darker than that of the Jews. Some of the town children were in danger of running under the feet of the huge animals that carried the oriental looking visitors. It was obvious that the whole company was intent on coming to her home and Mary instinctively ran to Jesus and, disregarding his muddy condition, lifted him to her bosom for protection. Jesus pointed quizzically at the approaching beasts and shouted to them in that peculiar language known only unto infants who have not yet learned to speak more than a few words.

The animals drew near and knelt submissively at the command of their masters who slid with surprising dignity from their backs. One of them approached Mary and with regal grace bowed low before her as though before some royal personage. He then explained that he and his two colleagues, together with their servants, had travelled from the east for many weeks across the burning desert in search of a king who had been born in the land of Judea. They were students of the stars and saw the star of a king in the skies above their own nation and dutifully followed it to Israel. They visited the palace of Herod in Jerusalem thinking that perhaps the new king would be found there, but unfortunately it was not so. Further enquiries suggested that the one they sought was born in fulfilment of some ancient prophecy which stated that Bethlehem was the place out of which would emerge a great king. The previous night the star had appeared again and seemed to be guiding them to the carpenter's shop in Bethlehem. So here they were. The eastern gentleman completed his oration and once more bowed low before the Jewish maiden and her little boy.

Mary clutched her baby to her breast and her eyes flooded with tears. The last year had been so uneventful that it was easy to forget the miraculous origins of her pregnancy and the wonder of her son's birth. Family life was so like a dream come true. The children were happy, Jesus was so cute and adored by all, and laughter filled their inauspicious home. She and Joseph were very much in love. They enjoyed their days, talked together through the quietness of the evenings, and made love while the children slept. The words of the foreigner were a prelude to reality. It all came rushing back like a flood. She should have known that normality could never be hers. The mud-covered infant in her arms was no ordinary child. Like the man said, He was a king, and she was faced with the fact that men of great wisdom and intellect had travelled the desert to pay Him homage. She bowed her head respectfully in acknowledgement of her visitors and apologetically invited them into her unpretentious home. She whispered to one of her neighbours to make haste and bring Joseph to the house.

It was a peculiar sight which met the eyes of the dusty carpenter as he ran into his house. Mary was sitting with Jesus on her lap. The boy had thick streaks of mud on his face and legs and he wore a delighted grin at being the centre of attention. A group of strangers, foreigners, impressively dressed in their native attire, were kneeling before the mother and child and the floor was strewn with gifts of gold, frankincense and myrrh. Mary introduced the noble visitors to her husband, giving him a brief account of how they had come to be in Bethlehem.

They lingered for several hours and, despite their obvious poverty, Mary and Joseph were the perfect hosts. They presented their visitors with the finest cuisine they could obtain and listened with fascination to the men's stories of desert travel and details of a distant culture so different from their own. They were nervous to discover that their little boy had been the subject of a discussion between these men and none other than King Herod himself and were even more disconcerted to discover that Herod had made specific request to be informed about the whereabouts of the child once it became known. Mary's heart fainted with fear. The cruelty and violence of which Herod was capable was no secret. This was the man who ordered the murder of his own wife, Miriamne, and killed three of his own sons through fear that they might usurp his throne. If these pilgrims from afar kept their word and reported their findings to the Palace then her son was in gravest danger. It was with a heart in turmoil that she waved farewell to her visitors and with much prayer for the protection of her Heavenly Father that she went to her bed.

It was a warm night in May and only the sound of distant crickets broke the silence. It was a long time before either Joseph or Mary fell asleep. They were unsettled. Anxiety filled their minds and their hearts were alert to danger. When Joseph finally succumbed to his weariness he dreamed of armies marching to battle and men, women and children being slaughtered by flashing swords and flying arrows. He saw city walls breached by creatures which had the bodies of men but the heads of wild beasts, with long forked tongues and eyes that burned with evil. He could hear the screams of the women and observed as blood flowed like a river down streets which were littered with the corpses of the slain. Then, standing above the scene of carnage he saw once more the angel of the Lord, suspended in the heavens and resplendent with the serenity which only belongs to those who know they have total control. He stood with sword drawn in his hand and spoke to Joseph as he had spoken to him on the night before Mary's return from Elizabeth.

"Arise Joseph, and take the young child and his mother, and flee into Egypt, and be thou there until I bring thee word: for Herod will seek the young child to destroy Him."

He woke with a start, his heart pounding. He was soaked with perspiration. Mary was fast asleep. The house was silent. He quietly rose up, pulled a cloak about him, and went outside into the cool chill of the night. Bethlehem was asleep. He searched the night sky as though looking for more guidance from infinity. A wolf howled in the distant hills. The old questions worked their way through his troubled brain. Had he really seen an angel? Was it just a bad dream because he went to sleep in the throes of anxiety? Was God telling him to flee to Egypt? What should he do?

"O God of Abraham, Isaac, and Jacob, please help me. Please show me if my dream was from you or a creation of my troubled mind. Did you send your angel to speak with me again? Please give to me a sign if it was you."

As he prayed a shooting star flashed across the clear night sky and evaporated into the horizon. He decided to wake Mary.

The young couple stood with their arms around each other and looked out into the night. He told her of his dream with full expectation that she would voice some negatives about a one hundred mile journey across a barren, rocky, dangerous desert. Instead she looked with incredulity into the face of her beloved. He could barely make out her features in the subdued light of the night sky, but he could see the light of the moon glistening on the tears which welled in her eyes. She was animated with a sense of urgency.

"Joseph, before I fell asleep tonight, a scripture came so vividly to my mind which I read long ago in the book of the prophet Hosea. It says, 'Out of Egypt have I called My Son'. I thought about its meaning and failed to understand its relevance, but now I see it. It is God's plan that we go immediately to Egypt for the protection of His Son. I believe that He brought the scripture to my mind as He did the one from Micah when I was afraid to make the journey from Nazareth to Bethlehem. Your dream was from our Father in heaven. We must go with haste, now Joseph, before it is too late."

They woke the children with promises of adventures galore in an exciting journey across the mountains. Joseph brought the trusty Dan from the adjoining field and well before dawn began to lighten the eastern sky over the Judean hills they were already on their way to Tekoa. Here they stopped and ate breakfast and purchased three more donkeys with some of the gold they had been given by the men from the east. They stocked up with food and water and as the sun climbed into the heavens they were on their way to Hebron. Meanwhile a divine visitation to the men from Arabia warning them not to return to Herod but to return home another way was met with humble acquiescence.

For three weeks the fragile caravan of donkeys travelled across the forbidding hills, uncharted valleys of rock and the rugged emptiness and grandeur of Sinai, miraculously unnoticed by marauding tribesmen and wild beasts. The heat was searing at the zenith of the day and the cold was equally devastating in the desert night, so they prayed for relief from the daytime heat and huddled together for warmth when darkness fell. Sometimes they travelled very early in the morning or very late in the evening and rested when they sheltered from the midday sun. They laughed, they wept, they shouted and they sang. Sometimes it all seemed too much and they wondered if they would make it through this barren world of rock, but they kept moving on. Finally they arrived at the border crossing at the River of Egypt and came to a city called Heliopolis. There was a large Jewish population in the city, the descendants of those who had escaped southwards from the Babylonian invasion of Israel by Nebuchadnezzar in 606 BC. They even had Jewish Synagogues and other examples of Jewish culture. It was reasonably easy for Joseph to find quite comfortable lodgings for his family and for the first time in his life, thanks to his eastern benefactors, he had the finances to pay his way without anxiety.

Further north the sword fell with bloody brutality. Herod's soldiers rampaged across Bethlehem and the surrounding area murdering every male baby under two years of age. Distraught mothers had their babies plucked from their breasts and screamed vainly for mercy as the heads of their young offspring were dashed against the rocks. Others were hacked in pieces by the edge of the sword or trampled to death by the boots of the soldiers. Many mothers also died in the holocaust as they threw themselves over their children to protect them from the wonton barbarity. The screams of pain and fear were horrendous and the merciless slaughter continued until not a child remained alive. The wailing of the bereaved floated across the hills of Bethlehem and the anguished sobbing of countless mothers could be heard long into the night. Many of them gathered at the tomb of Rachel to weep for their loss. They could hear the bones of the mother of Israel weeping for her children.

CHAPTER FIFTEEN

The sojourn of the Holy Family in Egypt was not an unpleasant one. The thriving Jewish community together with the presence of the ever dominating Roman influence made it almost home from home. They were treated kindly by the locals and Mary found herself able to relax in an atmosphere of security and safety which she had not fully experienced since the night of the conception. For this reason she suffered some disquiet when Joseph informed her of yet another angelic dream announcing that Herod was now dead and that it was time for them to return, not only to Israel, but to Nazareth. She did not welcome the exchange of this culture of quietness for the potential anxieties and inevitable tensions which would greet their appearance in her home town. She had learned, however, never to argue with divine direction. She knew that He who sees the end from the beginning and who holds the balance of time in His hands, seeing the past and the future as though they were present, always knows best. She had learned to trust and was prepared at all times to walk a difficult path to the right destination rather than the road of self-will which leads inexorably to destruction.

So she wound up her affairs in Heliopolis, packed their accumulated belongings, and prepared for the long journey home. Joseph was loathe to travel through Judea and the hill country because it was under the control of Herod's notoriously cruel son, Archelaus, who seemed to have inherited his father's wickedness. Following the death of Herod, who endured the most horrendous and painful end, the kingdom was divided between Archelaus and his younger and less violent brother Antipas who controlled the Galilee. So Mary found herself once more on the back of a donkey in a caravan at AL-Quantara which saw the beginning of the Mediterranean coast road known to the Romans as the Via Maris, or the Way of the Sea. The road ran northwards through Gaza and onwards to the valley of Jezreel, across the valley and then up the North West coast of Lake Galilee. From north Galilee it pushed still further North Eastward as far as Damascus. It was the ideal route for a family bound for Nazareth and afforded a great deal more security than the one they had traversed on their flight to Egypt. It was also interspersed with coastal towns and communities which provided ideal stop-off places to spend the nights.

It was a strange feeling as they turned left out of the valley of Jezreel and took the old familiar road into Nazareth. The years of absence had changed nothing: the same scattered houses in the familiar agricultural setting and the lush beauty of the hills standing guard over the community. And then the homely creak of the carpentry door as they nervously entered the home they had not seen for four years. Everything was exactly as they left it before their torturous journey to Bethlehem, except for the very thick layer of dust which lay like a transparent shroud over the contents. The ever-efficient Mary summed up the task before them in an instant and began dividing the chores between the children. Soon the house was bustling with activity. The cloak of dirt was removed from chairs and table and floor and soon they were able to sit down to a basic meal of cheese, olives and bread followed by fruit and nuts. It was like they had never been away.

The days following saw Joseph searching for business while Mary placed the older children in school. She then took the infant Jesus on a tour of the town, showing him the vineyards and the winepress, the olive trees, the wheat and the barley, all of which grew on fertile terraces cleverly cut into the south-facing slopes of the hills. She explained to him the wonders of nature and introduced him to the almonds and figs which grew in abundance around the edges of the town. She gave him a drink from the local spring and they climbed her favourite hill together from where she showed him the spectacular landscape and pointed out the historic landmarks of the region. These first impressions of Nazareth were embedded in the memory of Jesus and became the bedrock of knowledge from which came many of the parables with which he illustrated truth in the years of his public ministry. He was soon to be five years old and was already displaying a keen curiosity for everything around him and questions poured in a never-ending stream from his enquiring mind. He pleaded to help his father make stools and chairs. He wanted to know what was inside the thin wool-filled mattress which was his bed. He asked how grapes became wine, how birds knew how to make their nests and how eggs came to be inside a hen. How did they make the mud which insulated the inside of the stone walls of their house? The questions were without end. Mary found herself asking Joseph questions like, "Why do they mix ash into the dirt floor?" She wasn't really interested herself, but wanted to be ready if her young son challenged her with a question she could not answer.

Mary laughed every day at the antics of her child. He was a happy boy and often entertained the whole family with his cute and memorable observations. He was particularly moved by anything religious. Mary noticed how serious he became when Joseph called the family to prayer. He seemed to touch the Mezuzah, which always hung mysteriously on the doorpost of the entrance to the carpentry, with more reverence than the other children. He loved the Sabbath meal, the kindling of the Sabbath lamp, and he always sat enthralled when Mary shared with him stories of the miracles which God had done for His people. He loved the varied celebrations of the Jewish feasts. He was fascinated with Chanukah, the illumination festival in the wintertime when each succeeding night increasing numbers of candles were lit in the home. His mother deliberately built the excitement on the first night with the lighting of the first lone candle, and then made much of the nightly illumination of succeeding candles until by the eighth night the whole room glowed with lambent beauty. It was great fun, as was the celebration of the salvation which came to the Jews through Queen Esther at the feast of Purim when everyone laughed and told stories and sang together. The feast he loved best, however, was the feast of Tabernacles when everybody camped outside for a whole week in home-made leafy booths. It was like a huge harvest festival and always left indelible memories in the minds of the young.

They were happy years, obviously not trouble free, but Mary was thankful for everything. There were still some hostile looks from maliciously minded individuals who would not forget the suspicious circumstances surrounding the birth of Mary's child; even some nasty name-calling of Jesus, but she was wise enough to know that in the final issue it would do him no harm. If her feeling of apprehension for the future was ever realised then she knew that he needed a few knocks as a child to put strength and endurance into his character. So she only gave him the motherly hugs when she felt that he had received the benefit of adversity. She was always there for him nevertheless. When he fell and grazed his knee she was there to wash it clean and apply the soothing ointment. When he was sick with childhood fevers she cradled him in her arms and wiped his burning brow. And she prayed for him continually. Early in the morning this Godly woman rose to seek God, ever conscious of the almost unbearable responsibility which she had been given, and every night when the children and Joseph were asleep she knelt in the corner and quietly wept her burden back to God.

To her also fell the responsibility of the pre-school education of her son. She taught him the commandments which God gave to Moses and encouraged him to commit them to memory. They also memorised together many of David's psalms, often singing them as a family at the end of a meal as they sat around the fire. She read him passages from the scriptures which she knew were beyond his understanding, but he sat in the presence of truth as though its very spirit washed his soul. From time to time she read from the writings of the prophet Isaiah, passages which she knew were applicable to his future, and sometimes she choked on the words as she read them and he would hold her arm with both his hands and say, "Mummy what's wrong? What do those words mean that make you cry?" She would tell him that they were the tears that a woman sheds for the love of her son.

When Jesus turned six he graduated from his mother's knee to the school which annexed the Synagogue, an occasion which coincided with the birth of Mary's second son James. It was an emotional time as it seemed to her that she was giving one son away whilst receiving another. She adored her new baby but wept to see Jesus leave for his first day at school. His teacher was the Chazzan, or officer of the Synagogue. The accommodation was basic, no chairs or benches, and both teacher and pupils either stood or sat on the floor in a half circle. The teaching was both religious and moral, training the children to abstain from all things evil, to always speak the truth, to be kind and obedient, disciplined and diligent to study. For the first four years of school the scriptures were the only text book. From ages ten to fifteen the traditional law, the Mishnah, was taught, but for the young Jesus it was the scriptures, beginning with the book of Leviticus, which stimulated both intellect and curiosity. Both at home and at school the sacred text became his meat and drink.

Jesus grew to love the occasional excursions to Bethsaida to visit his aunt Salome and his cousin James. His uncle Zebedee often took the two boys out on his boat and the young Jesus loved to trail his fingers in the water as they sped across the lake. Sometimes James' best friend Simon, brother of Andrew, accompanied them. His father Jonas was a fisherman like Zebedee and Simon was really clever. He knew how the sails worked and sometimes he actually went out fishing with his father. He could swim like a fish. Sometimes Jesus wished that he and his family could live by the sea. He didn't really have many friends in Nazareth and his brothers and sisters were not always kind to him, but he loved his three friends in Bethsaida. A bond existed between these very young boys which seemed deeper than a mere family connection.

Mary and Salome made the best of these times together and talked, as sisters do, about their hopes and fears. Salome told Mary about the vision which she saw on the day of her wedding anniversary when, whilst sailing the lake, she had a premonition of the violent death of her son James, and Mary told her of her fears for Jesus in the light of ancient prophecy. They tried to console each other with reassurances which neither of them really believed. They soon came to realise that such discourses were not edifying, in fact were counterproductive, and Mary decided that it was perhaps better to just speak together of happier things because every time they talked of possible future gloom, a cold spiritual mist closed in around them, as though their conversation was being overheard by hostile and sinister forces interested only in their demise.

The highlight of the year was the annual trip to Jerusalem to celebrate the feast of Passover. Mary always used the opportunity to leave a few days early in order to visit Elizabeth and Zacharias at Bet Hakerem. Jesus loved to play with his cousin John on the dust slope of the hill outside their simple home. John was a bold, tough little fellow, not as tall as his younger cousin, but strong and assertive. The two boys got on well together and Mary's heart rejoiced as she watched the forming of a friendship which she believed would change the world. After a couple of days at Bet Hakerem they all left together and attached themselves to the passing pilgrims for the final trek into Jerusalem for the feast.

Jerusalem was always awash with people and excitement rippled across the sea of visitors who came from across Israel to celebrate the deliverance of their nation from slavery in Egypt some 1500 years before. Passover was originally a one day holiday, but grew and developed into a full week of festivities, Passover day itself, of course, being the most important. This was the day that the Jews in Israel celebrated the time in their history when their forefathers in Egypt, on the instructions given by Moses, slaughtered a lamb for each household and applied the animal's blood to the doorposts and lintels of their homes. As God's judgment descended on the Egyptian homes, the Jewish families safely ate roast lamb under the protection of the symbolic blood before leaving the slavery of Egypt for ever. To commemorate this amazing historic deliverance the pilgrims ate unleavened bread sandwiches filled with a portion of the paschal lamb mixed with bitter herbs. After the meal thousands of people went in procession up the hill to the Temple singing the Hallel psalms as they went, entering the Temple Courts with great rejoicing and praying for the coming of the long-expected Messiah. Mary's youthful spirit exulted in the surge of religious fervour produced by these events. It was as though all the Synagogues across the land became one in this massive and holy convocation and the combined atmospheres of a thousand places of worship transported her to the seventh heaven as she stood on the sacred Mount Zion with her motherly arms firmly holding her precious children to her skirts.

On the second morning of the feast Joseph and Mary always took their children to watch the priests descend into the Kidron Valley to cut the first sheaf of newly-ripened barley. This they then carried back up to the Temple to offer it as a wave offering of thanksgiving to God.

So year by year the family from Nazareth made the journey to Jerusalem with crowds of friends and family, prolonging the holiday by making the return journey as enjoyable as their time in the city. Mary was protective of her children, but especially of James because he was the youngest, and of Jesus, because he was Jesus. It was on their visit to the Passover feast in the thirteenth year of her firstborn son that Mary had a revelation of this celebration which would change her view of it forever. They made their customary visit to the home of Elizabeth, travelled together to the city and celebrated the Passover meal as usual. They sang their way to the Temple and stood with the rest of the people as they prayed for the coming of the Messiah. It was then that her son suddenly slipped his hand into her own and she felt him tremble. She turned and looked him in the eyes. She thought how grown up he looked. He would soon be taller than her. For a moment she misread his expression for one of religious awe, but then realised it was the look of fear. She felt alarm.
"What's wrong Jesus? Why do you fear so?"
"I don't know mother," he replied. "I feel strange. You know how our fathers killed the lambs in Egypt to bring deliverance to the people; something like that will never happen again will it? All those dying lambs! All that blood! I feel afraid, mother. I feel like I can taste the blood."

The words of her boy went like a sword into the heart of his mother. In an instant this happy feast of celebration and rejoicing was changed into an odious prophecy of blood and pain and death. She knew in a flash of revelation that the events of long ago were merely a type of an event soon to be when the Messiah would offer Himself as the paschal lamb, slain in God's plan from the foundation of the world, for the deliverance of mankind from slavery to sin. She would not be singing then, and she should not be singing now. Guilt gripped her soul. She was rejoicing over the death of her beloved son. She turned and embraced Jesus with a passion he had not felt from her before. She held him for a long time in the arms of unutterable love, afraid to let him go lest the future steal him away. Then she summoned her will and looked reassuringly into his face. "You have nothing to fear, my son," she smiled. "Our Heavenly Father will be with You always."

The rest of the feast was an anticlimax for Mary. No matter how much she tried she found it impossible to see the Passover in the same way and she knew that she never would, not for as long as she lived. Her understanding was quickened. It was no longer the celebration of a past event but the type of a sacrifice yet to be offered. The Passover feast had become her enemy. Jesus was not the same either. The little boy appeared suddenly changed, thoughtful and mature beyond his years. Whatever he had felt on Passover night had changed him also. He seemed a step removed from her and she could no longer properly reach him. As the group of excited families headed out of Jerusalem at the close of the holiday she confided her feelings and fears to Joseph. She was concerned for her son's sombre mood and felt that she needed more wisdom to handle it.

"Maybe he just needs time on his own Mary. You do tend to be a little over protective. He's at a difficult age. I think you should just let him be with his friends. Give him some space and I'm sure he'll be fine."

He put his strong arm around her shoulder. He knew that she would find that very difficult to do. Mothers don't like it when their children start to become adults.

When they stopped for the night and campfires burned like beacons across the hills Mary took her husband's arm.

"Where is Jesus, Joseph? Have you seen him? Do you think he's safe?"

"I'm sure he's having a wonderful time with his cousin John," Joseph said with not a flicker of concern. "The two of them are probably climbing the rocks."

Mary turned away. "I'm just going to find Elizabeth. She will know where John is. I won't be long."

Joseph smiled his resignation as Mary walked briskly across the camp to see her beloved cousin. She returned within a few minutes with a look of deep concern etched into her face.

"Joseph, John is with his mother and father and none of them have seen Jesus since we left Jerusalem this morning. Where can he be?"

Her voice rose with agitation and self-recrimination. "We should never have left him. Oh my poor boy. What has become of him?"

Tears were flowing freely down her face and she was shaking to the rhythm of the adrenalin surges which pulsated through her body. Joseph lovingly took hold of her arm but she brushed it angrily aside.

"I should never have listened to you," she chided.

She ran off amongst the people with panic seizing her senses. She shouted his name across the noisy camp, but her shouting was in vain. He was nowhere to be found. People stood wide-eyed as she demanded to know if they had seen a boy called Jesus. An elderly man from Nazareth made an attempt to restrain her, but she would tolerate no hindrance to her mission. Blind fear was causing her to lose control and it took Joseph to eventually calm her down. With a display of controlled indignation he gripped her shoulders and demanded her attention.

"Mary, this is doing no good. You will not find Jesus this way. If you will just be calm I will contact everyone here and if we fail to find him we will start back to Jerusalem."

It was a very long night and Mary, though more controlled, felt sick with worry. Joseph appeared not to worry, but inside he felt the heavy stone of anxiety in his stomach. Dawn was lighting the distant hills before they mounted donkeys and headed back towards Jerusalem. Elizabeth agreed to take the children to her home to be collected later so the two of them made good progress and reached the city by midday. They went straight to the lodging house where they had stayed for the feast but the kindly old landlord had not seen Jesus since the family departed the previous morning. They went to the Temple, but, even though the feast was over, people were milling everywhere and it was an impossible task. They walked the streets of

Jerusalem until their legs ached and their hearts fainted. Despair killed their hopes and as the night fell they returned to their old lodgings with weeping souls. They prayed long into the night, pleading with God to forgive their negligence and asking for guidance as to where he might be found. They slept fitfully for a couple of hours before resuming their search at daybreak. They began again asking people if they had seen a boy of about twelve years old but received only disapproving shakes of the head in response. Eventually they accosted a Rabbi on the steps of the Temple who told them that he had seen a boy matching their description asking questions of some of his colleagues less than an hour before. He sent them in the right direction and with hope rising and hearts pumping they pushed their way through the crowd.

Mary saw her son across the crowded court. He was sitting with a group of religious doctors and lawyers discussing the Law of Moses and its implications for modern society. It was a strange sight, a twelve year old boy in deep conversation with learned Rabbis. By the expressions on the faces of his older companions they were more than impressed with his questions and contributions. She pushed her way through the people with relief and anger alternately seizing her pent-up emotions. Tears of joy spilled onto lips tight with indignation. She reached his side, gripped his arm, and the words poured from her lips with unbridled, maternal passion.

"Jesus, where have you been? How could you? How dare you put your father and me through three days of worry and fear? We have been looking for you everywhere. I allowed you to be with your friends and you abused my trust. We got a full day's journey on the road to Nazareth and then we couldn't find you. We have come all the way back. We didn't know where you were. I thought that you were dead, or carried away by wicked men. Why did you do it Jesus? Jesus! Oh thank God I have found you!"

She threw her arms around him and held him to her breast. Her tears dampened his face but he said nothing until finally she stepped back. The doctors of religion were surveying the scene with professional detachment. Jesus looked from his mother to his father, who had not yet spoken a single word. He had a controlled but bemused expression on his face. Then Jesus replied to his mother with words which sounded impudent, but were tempered with such sweet sincerity as to make them mature rather than disrespectful.

"Why did you not understand that I must be about My Father's business?"

Mary's instinct was to react with maternal indignance, but before the protest could surface the memory of who he was stayed her lips. She could hear again the words of the angel, "He shall be great, and shall be called the Son of the Highest." The realisation dawned that she was encountering for the first time the authority of God in human flesh. The anger evaporated in an instant and was replaced by an overwhelming desire to kneel at the feet of her own son. She stood in stunned silence not knowing what to do. Then Jesus stood to his feet, politely begged to be excused from his distinguished companions, and kindly took his mother's arm. They merged into the passing throng and Jesus was once more the submissive twelve year old son of Mary. The matter was never spoken of again.

Throughout the rest of his young life in Nazareth Jesus was the perfectly obedient son, never showing dissent or any hint of rebellion but maintaining an attitude of willing submissiveness at all times, but when in later years Mary told her story and recounted her experiences in the upbringing of the Christ it was the incident when he was twelve years old which was the overwhelming memory of the time, not just because of the trauma surrounding it, but because it was the moment she first glimpsed the true identity of her son.

That historic Passover feast in the thirteenth year of our Lord was also the occasion of the conception of the one who was destined be called the beloved disciple of Jesus in years to come. Zacharias and Salome with their son James were also present in Jerusalem for the celebration of the Passover and it was during that time that their second child was conceived and nine months later Salome gave birth to another son. They called him John. He was chosen to play a massive part in the life and welfare of Mary, the mother of Jesus.

CHAPTER SIXTEEN

Mary passionately loved her husband. The passing years drew them closer together. By the time Jesus reached his eighteenth birthday the rest of the family, Justus, Simon, Judas and the two girls, had flown the nest. Jesus spent most of His time either working in the carpentry, or walking in the hills talking to His other Father, or sitting on the grassy slopes reading and studying the scriptures. Mary and Joseph had more time to spend together and they enjoyed it like a couple of teenagers tasting the fruit of first love. They laughed together, and prayed together. They walked together through the olive groves and the vineyards in the cool of the day and they loved each other long into the night. Mary loved the security of his strong arms, the lingering smell of the olive wood in his skin, the smile in his eyes as he gazed into hers. She could never imagine life without him.

Jesus loved His father also, as did his younger brother James. The three of them were the best of friends. They chattered endlessly, often engaging in boisterous wrestling matches on the carpentry floor, Mary feigning indignation as they emerged covered from head to foot in sawdust. On days when they had no work they laughed their way to the top of the surrounding hills and sat for hours in endless competitions seeing who could throw a stone nearest to a marker stone without knocking it, or who could score a hit on a nearby tree. They returned in the evenings starving hungry and Mary would feed them with home-made cheese, fish, vegetables, eggs and fruit, washed down with local wine. Then they would sit and tell stories of times past and present until candles burned low and weariness gave way to sleep.

It was in the month of May, in the nineteenth year of her eldest son, that Mary sensed one of her feelings of foreboding as she took to her bed. It had been a pleasant day and all seemed well, yet she had a strange sense of apprehension in her heart. She embraced her sleeping husband with a hunger for security, listening to his steady breathing for reassurance that all was well. She heard the howl of a wild dog somewhere in the hills and it triggered a shiver down her spine. The night was warm for early summer but she felt a chill in her soul. Jesus and James were both asleep. She drifted into a fitful sleep and dreamed of the dragon. How she hated that vile creature with its evil eyes and ugly teeth. It lowered its repulsive form over her body and she lifted her hands to defend herself, but the monster seemed undeterred. She could feel the heat of its scaly flesh and smell the stench of its foul breath as it rolled its eyes and came closer. Then it fastened its jaws around her chest and she felt excruciating pain as it crushed the life from her body. She woke with a cry of anguish, perspiration seeping from every pore of her skin. She shuddered with relief that she was still alive, but the dreadful feeling of pending horror was overwhelming. She had slept late and Joseph was already gone into his workshop. Jesus was also missing and James was away to school. She washed and dressed and brushed her hair, all the time whispering a prayer to her Heavenly Father that all might be well. Familiar words from the sayings of Isaiah the Prophet filled her mind, "Thou wilt keep him in perfect peace whose mind is stayed on thee." She calmed her troubled heart and moved towards the carpentry. A wave of apprehension swept over her as she pushed open the door. The scene which met her anxious eyes confirmed the worst of her fears. Something was terribly wrong.

Joseph was lying sprawled across the earthen floor and Jesus was crouched down at his side, cradling His fathers head in his arms. He was profusely weeping, deep unintelligible sobs rising from the depths of His bowels, shoulders heaving with anguish. The face of His dead father was wet with His tears. No word passed between them as Mary knelt by her son's side. One arm was stretched around the shoulder of the living whilst her other hand gently stroked the face of the dead. Her beloved husband was gone, snatched away from her with no opportunity even to say goodbye. He was only forty-four years old and she was now a widow of only thirty-four. The world caved in around both mother and son. Their sense of loss was indescribable. They knelt together with their beloved for what seemed an eternity. Their tears ebbed and flowed. They could hear children playing in the street, oblivious to their pain. Mary began to rehearse what she would say to James and her older children.

Jesus was like a young man in a dream as He walked the streets of Nazareth to break the sad news to His family and friends and to inform the Rabbi of the death of His father. It was accepted in Jewish culture that friends would rally round and make arrangements for the funeral of a neighbour, which would normally take place on the same day as the death. They would come and bathe the body according to the standards of Kvod-ha-met, giving due honour to the remains of their friend, wrap it in the Takhirkhin and prepare it for burial. The whole funeral event was organised to be a celebration of life rather than an occasion for sorrowing. The period of mourning would take place during the week following.

So it was, late that tragic afternoon, that Mary followed her husband's bier to the burial caves on the outskirts of the town. His body was wrapped from head to toe in a white burial shroud and placed face upwards on the crudely constructed stretcher. She held her head high with dignity, but her heart was crushed with sorrow. She joined in the chanting of the psalms at the burial site, but she was not singing on the inside. She found it difficult to understand why God would snatch him away like this. Her sense of foreboding regarding the future of her son grew with the passing years. She now faced that future alone, stripped so suddenly of the support and comfort of her soul mate. She glanced across at Jesus. She knew how much He was hurting and how difficult it would be for Him to work alone in the carpentry feeling everyday the emptiness left by His departed father. For now, however, He was acting with a maturity beyond His years, caring and comforting His older brothers and sisters, and, quite literally supporting young James like a father would support his son. James came and clung to his mother's arm and she held his head against her breast, stroking the back of his head, a silent reassurance of her love. Over his shoulder she could see Jesus standing alone, silhouetted against the evening sky, gazing into the mouth of the cave where His father lay. She then experienced one of those strange inexplicable glimpses into the future. It was as though she saw a somewhat older Jesus standing before another burial cave. He was weeping, she knew not why, but she heard no sound. He seemed to give instructions for the cave stone to be removed and then she watched as He lifted His hands to form a haler around His mouth. He appeared to shout, although again there was no sound. She gasped as from the tomb before Him there emerged a body, Takhirkhin still in place. He had called a man back from death! Helpers rushed to free the man from the encumbering shroud and then He was walking, running, leaping with joy, and embracing her son with grateful praise. The vision faded, and the young man Jesus was walking towards her, arms slightly open to receive her. She walked into his embrace, and He gazed into her eyes. They glistened with tears.

"I am so sorry, mother, but it is not yet time."

He knew what she had seen. It was as though He could read her thoughts. The man who stood before her would one day raise the dead, but too late to help the man who had held Him in his arms as a baby, too late to repay the gentle servant who had given his all to bring Him to maturity.

Mary walked slowly back towards the carpentry with her two boys, one on each arm, and in her heart she whispered "Forgive me, Lord! Thy will, not mine, be done!"

CHAPTER SEVENTEEN

Following the death of her husband Mary devoted herself entirely to the care of her two sons, giving herself more to prayer and communion with God that she might know His wisdom. It was difficult to care for Jesus because He instantly assumed the role of carer Himself, watching for His mother's every need, every mood change, every sign of distress, and moving in to minister to her needs with utter devotion. He loved His mother like His very breath. It was difficult for Him to carry the responsibility of the business and to cope with working alone, but she never once saw Him troubled or agitated, and He did his sorrowing away from her so as not to cause her anxiety. As the months passed she discerned the deepening relationship He had with His Heavenly Father and began to realise that the removal of Joseph was driving Him to a closer walk with God. Perhaps Joseph had taken Him as far as he could and his premature removal was all part of his sacrifice to bring Emmanuel to the world. How wise were the ways of the Almighty, but how painful for mere mortals to endure!

James was doing well at school, but was anxious to leave so that he might help his brother in the workshop. On his days off he was learning fast how to use the tools and Jesus seemed to enjoy teaching him. James loved his elder brother with a passion. He was deeply religious, a believer in the law and the prophets, and lived his life accordingly. His sense of righteousness and fair play earned him the life long nick name "James the Just." He believed that Jesus was the promised Messiah and questioned both Him and his mother about the meaning of scripture. Mary watched the commitment of the younger brother to the older with a warm heart. She was so pleased that there was no flicker of jealousy or envy in James. He was a lovely boy. It would delight the heart of any mother to see two brothers so inseparable, so selfless in their attitude to each other, each serving the other with unquestionable respect. She did sometimes feel that James' religious fervour bordered on the fanatical. He decided that he wanted to take the Nazarite vow, like his cousin John. It meant that he would never touch a dead body, never take strong drink, and never cut his hair, as a sign that he was separated to God and His service. Jesus argued that you could serve God from the heart without external symbols, but James insisted that he would like to show the commitment of his heart by the taking of the vows. So his hair grew long, the envy of many of the girls in Nazareth, and he grew taller than his older brother. The two of them paid frequent visits to see their cousins who now lived in Capernaum. Salome's son James was now a powerful fishermen and skilled boatmen and was already seeking to teach his six-year old brother John the rudiments of the art. He and his friends, Simon and Andrew, dominated the fishing industry on the lake. It was a wonderful change from the carpentry to go out in the boats with the others, although Mary constantly worried for his safety. Jesus placed his strong hands on His mother's waist and lifted her high into the air and, grinning from ear to ear, scolded her for her worrying.

"Mother, mother!" he said. "Shall not He who cares for the animals in the field and the sparrows on the house top care for His own? Oh you of little faith!" His eyes flashed with mischief as He swung her round and lowered her gently to her feet. She returned His smile and playfully smacked his shoulder.

Mary never stopped missing her dear husband. Oft-times she would turn to embrace him in the night and feel the cold emptiness of his absence. The passing years made things no easier. Jesus and James were running a competent business which meant that she was financially viable, but she was ever more conscious that the change would come. The true identity of her eldest son was ever before her and she knew that at a pre-arranged moment up ahead all their lives would change. She sensed that the loneliness she felt at the loss of her husband was only the beginning. She was also to endure the loss of her son. In fact she had a strange premonition, one which she chose to ignore, that she was going to lose both her sons.

It was the day before Jesus' twenty-fifth birthday that she heard the sad news of the passing of her dear cousin Elizabeth. It was mid-morning on a cool autumnal morning that the door opened and her nephew John stood framed in the entrance. He was a rough-looking character, sporting a full beard and masses of unkempt dark brown hair. He was of medium height, with strong muscular arms and legs, and shoulders which gave the impression of being too wide for his height. He wore a tunic cloaked with a loose-fitting coarse brown mantle tied at the waist with a wide leather belt and tough leather sandals which had seen better days. He had the most striking eyes which, though somewhat clouded with sorrow, had the piercing qualities of a man fired with passion and belief. John was a radical, outspoken and fearless, a man who loved God and righteousness, despised the niceties of life, and was prepared to suffer in the cause of truth. He strode across the room without uttering a word and embraced his aunt in silence. She sensed him weeping softly into her shoulder and knew instinctively that his aged mother was gone.

"She is better now John," she whispered. "She has departed here, but arrived there. She rejoices in the presence of her Lord. Did she not love Him with all her heart, and serve Him so faithfully?

He stepped back and those fiery eyes flashed like gemstones from his hairy face.

"So she did Mary, so she did! And do you know what she said to me before she died? She gripped my hand and said, 'John, you must prepare the way for your cousin Jesus. Listen to the voice of God and He will guide you in what you must do. Tell Mary the time will not be long, and the Messiah shall be revealed'."

It was with a heart full of apprehensive wonderment that Mary served the meal that evening to three very special young men. She listened with interest to their debate about the future of Israel, the presence of the Roman occupiers, the defiant nationalism, but above all she saw the commitment of all three to the Will of the God of Abraham. They frequently laughed as they ate, sorrow and grief forgotten for a while as they teased Mary about the way she carried the food to the table. After the meal she sat in the corner and quietly promised her Heavenly Father that she would do her best to always be available to help Elizabeth's son. How like his late father he was, the same prominent nose, the same rolling gait, the same resonant voice. He was the prophet called to prepare the way for the Christ. He was the road builder, the preparer of men's hearts, the servant preceding his Lord, the lightening before the thunder. She suddenly felt his loneliness. He had nobody. His father and mother were gone. He had no brothers and sisters. She yearned to be his comforter.

"John, what are your plans now?" she asked. "We would love so much to have you come and live with us. You could help Jesus and James to build the business and ….." Her words were drowned out by the laughter of her nephew. He raised his hands in protest. "What? Me, a carpenter? Why Mary you would have chairs without legs and roofs that leak water. I thank you so much for offering and it would be wonderful to stay with you all, but I could never live here." He paused and became thoughtful and serious. "I like to be alone. I like to walk in wide-open spaces and listen to the voice of God. I feel His presence in the rugged hills of Judea. I have an inclination to just go and live rough in the wilderness."

"John", she protested, "you must not do that. Your dear mother would never forgive me if I stood by and allowed you to do such a thing."

John smiled kindly. "You worry too much Mary. I must go where I feel to go. Perhaps it is the divine will that I live in the desert. Who knows? Maybe it is in the wilderness that I will live, and preach, and one day die."

For a second she opened her mouth to remonstrate with him, but as she did so the words of the prophet flooded her mind: "Prepare ye the way of the Lord, make straight in the desert a highway for our God." Her words froze in her throat with the realisation that this strange-looking young man was the fulfilment of this 600 year old prophecy and that he was right; his work was to be done in the desert. She must not, dare not, stand in his way.

Long after the men were asleep Mary mused over the future of her sons and nephew. One of them she knew was born to be the Jewish Messiah, and James, although she, of course, had no idea, was destined to become the first Bishop of the Jerusalem Church, and the other was to precede them both with his powerful brief ministry in the desert. She pictured John with his long hair blowing in the wind, his eyes blazing with passion, his hand raised to emphasise his words and the enemies he would make through his outspoken manner. She closed her eyes and slipped into the mode of perception and revelation which often provided her with a visionary taste of things to come and saw him standing waist deep in the river whilst people queued on the banks to be baptised. She saw Jesus there in the line and watched as John appeared reluctant to baptise Him. Then she saw her son dipped beneath the cold water and she knew John's work was done. Then she saw a cold harsh-looking fortress in a desert place and her nephew crouched like a sick animal in a stinking cave. She saw a maiden dancing, and she saw the flash of a sword, and she saw a bloody head on a silver platter.

CHAPTER EIGHTEEN

It was another five years before Mary's preview of the baptism of Jesus by John in the River Jordan came to pass. Jesus and James spent the time working hard with their hands, whilst John lived adventurously in the desert of Judea. He wore a crudely made camel skin coat and lived on a diet of locusts and wild honey. After living in this manner for three years he began to attract attention and visitors began excursions into the wilderness to listen to his unique preaching. He declared that the Messiah was at hand and called upon the people to repent and be baptised for the remission of their sins. He set up a station for baptism close to Bethabara near to where the Jordan entered the Dead Sea. Mary heard that her young nephew John, now seventeen years old, and his friend Andrew son of Zebedee were regular visitors to the Jordan to listen to John preach, and that they had been baptised. For some reason Jesus and James did not yet show any inclination to visit their cousin.

Jesus seemed to suddenly change shortly after he turned thirty. He appeared restless, and Mary noticed him sitting alone for hours with a faraway look in his eyes. She was troubled. In her heart she knew that the time had come. For thirty years she had experienced and enjoyed the indescribable privilege and honour of living with the Son of God. She had tasted the purity of His person, the perfection of His untarnished character, but she always knew that He was on loan to her. She knew that the day would come when He would leave and the preaching of

John the Baptist was bringing that day ever closer. Now Jesus was awake for hours in the night talking to His Heavenly Father. He rarely spoke to her about His true calling, but she knew that He was more aware of it now than He had ever been. It came as no surprise when late one night He asked to speak with her and His brother.

"You both know that I am not on earth to be a carpenter," He began. "I am here to do the will of the One who sent me. He has called me to bring a message of hope to the world. I am not clear about the way He is leading me or what He expects of me in the future, but I do know that I should visit my cousin John down in Bethabara. More than that I do not know but I will be leaving first thing in the morning."

Mary swallowed hard and blinked back her tears. She had known for thirty years that this day would come, but now it had arrived she was still not fully prepared. She did not utter a word but slowly rose to her feet and embraced her son. She clung to Him for several minutes because she knew that from this night their relationship would change. She would never embrace Him like this again. Her son was going to become her Lord; flesh of her flesh was to be clothed with the Spirit of the Almighty. He would always be her son, but from this night she would see and honour him as Emmanuel, the Son of God. She kissed Him with the pure passion of maternal love and turned away with tears streaming down her face. She slept fitfully and awakened with the first paling of the dawn. She hurried from her room in the hope of seeing Him one more time before He left, but He had already slipped away, hoping to save His dear mother further parting pain. James collected his tools and went to work as usual, but Mary felt the sadness in his heart. She knew that he wanted to go with his brother. What's more, she knew that he would. It was just a matter of time.

As the weeks passed she longed for news of Jesus. All she heard was that He went to the Jordan and insisted that John baptise Him, but after that there was no information whatsoever. He seemed to have disappeared from the face of the earth. James wanted to go and search for Him, but Mary insisted that he remain where he was.
"Wherever He is, His Father will care for him," she said. She prayed for Him without ceasing. She had an overwhelming awareness of Jesus struggling against supernatural forces of evil. When she prayed she sensed a terrifying danger for her son and for the purposes of God. The dragon loomed again, desirous, by any means, of taking the life of her son before He could fulfil His ministry. She sensed the minions of hell, armies of demons, provoking, challenging, tempting, and tormenting her son, and she prayed that, wherever He was, the Father of Lights would strengthen His resolve, preserve His faithfulness, and protect Him from the dragon's mouth.

Two months after His departure Mary and James, together with Joseph, Simon, Judas, Esther, and Tamar and their families, were invited to the wedding of a nephew, the son of Cleopas, the brother of her late husband, in Cana, just a few miles from Nazareth. There was still no news of Jesus, and Mary had been forced to commit Him entirely to the Father and refuse to worry. The sun was hot, but Mary always enjoyed walking in the countryside. She felt at peace with the beauty of nature. She could see the fingerprints of God on the hills, and the perfection of His handiwork in the delicate summer flowers that garnished the grassy slopes. She could smell the perfume of His presence in the morning air, and her heart exulted with praise to the God of all creation.

It was just before noon when the group entered Cana and made for the home of Cleopas and his wife Mary. Mary saw the familiar form of Jesus from fifty metres away. He was sitting on a low stone wall outside the house with two young men who He had brought with Him from the Jordan, Philip and Nathaniel. She ran towards Him with undisguised relief. He stood and smiled His welcome and He embraced her warmly, but she had been correct that last night in Nazareth, it was not the same. He was different, like He was twice removed from her, living on another plane, strangely pre-occupied, in touch with another world. She desperately wanted to know where He had been for the last number of weeks and why she had felt so troubled about Him, but she knew better than to ask. She instinctively knew that whatever had been going on, it was between Him and His Father.

The wedding went well until they unfortunately ran out of wine. The host was most embarrassed, but had no way of replenishing his stocks so late in the day. Mary watched him engaged in whispered, animated conversation with his servants, but saw the gesture of hopelessness that came at the end of it. She then moved on impulse, rose from her seat, and approached Jesus. She had never seen Him perform a miracle, indeed He had never done a miracle, but she walked across to him and said, "They have no wine!"

The answer came as a sharp reminder that the future ministry of Jesus would be guided and controlled by God himself and would not in any way be affected by the wishes of any third party, not even His mother.

Jesus replied, "Woman, what have I to do with thee, mine hour is not yet come."

He had, at that moment, no direction from His Father to do anything. His words stung like salt in an open wound, but she shrugged off the hurt with remarkable ease and walked slowly across to the servants who stood in a concerned group in the corner of the room. She felt an unaccustomed boldness, a confidence that she was doing the right thing. She believed that it was the hour and that all it needed was for someone to make the challenge of faith. She was prepared to do it. She spoke quietly but firmly to the servants, inclining her head towards her son for identification. "Whatever He tells you to do, just do it!"

She watched attentively as Jesus sat for several minutes, troubled and thoughtful, before slowly rising to His feet and approaching the stewards. She saw their amazed expressions and the way they glanced across at her for reassurance. She smiled her affirmation and they nervously left the room. She watched as they returned several minutes later with several large pots of water and, again looking across for her moral support, began to pour it out to the governor of the feast. Mary gasped with reverent astonishment as she saw the water turn red as it ran from the water pot into the silver goblet, no longer water but the very best of wine. Her heart raced with the realisation that it had begun. The Son of God, her son, was revealed!

The following day Jesus left for Capernaum accompanied by Philip, Nathaniel, his brother James and of course his mother. Mary was determined that whatever was happening she was going to be a part of it. What she witnessed over the next few weeks exceeded her wildest expectations. The miracle at Cana was the launching pad for the miraculous. Fevers were cured, cripples walked, lepers were cleansed, the blind received their sight and crowds of people thronged the Synagogues wherever Jesus went. The news of this sensational preacher who had previously worked as a carpenter in the despised town of Nazareth spread throughout Israel. People in their thousands flocked to hear His message, bringing with them their sick and infirm relatives for healing. Some were saying that the Messiah had come.

CHAPTER NINETEEN

Salome heard the amazing stories concerning Jesus from her two sons. John had followed his cousin, John the Baptist, for some time and was present when he announced Jesus to be "The Lamb of God who takes away the sins of the world." He told his brother James and together they acknowledged Jesus as their Messiah. They had now forsaken their fishing business to follow Him, along with their close friends Simon and Andrew. Salome was worried about the business, especially as Zebedee was not well and was now semi-retired. She was, however, deeply moved by what she heard. She loved Jesus like He was her own son and she could truthfully say that she had never seen a flaw in His character. He was selfless and kind, always righteous in His dealings and His profound love for God was the outstanding feature of His life. She was drawn to go and find Him and her sons and to offer her services to their ministry, but it was hard to leave her aging husband even for a short period. After a valiant attempt to quench her conviction she spoke with Zebedee and they decided together that she should at least make the visit and see how she felt. He had tears in his tired eyes as he took her in his arms to bid her farewell. Something deep within told him that this was no passing fad. He knew that it was possible that it would be some time before she returned but if Jesus really was the promised Messiah he did not wish to stand in her way.

She found them in Capernaum. Jesus was using Simon's house as a base for His ministry and they had returned from a tour of Galilean cities just two days before her arrival. Her sister Mary was thrilled to see her and they chatted for hours about recent events, Mary telling her in detail about the amazing miracles that were flowing from the hands of her son. The two women took over the arrangements for feeding the group which had grown to quite a sizable family. Jesus had appointed twelve men to be His closest helpers. In addition to Simon (who He had surnamed Peter) and his brother Andrew, there were of course Salome's sons, James and John, Philip and Nathanael, the two whom Salome met at the wedding, also Matthew, a tax gatherer, Thomas, James the son of Alphaeus, Simon Zelotes, Judas, the son of Joseph the carpenter, and the future traitor, Judas Iscariot. Mary did wonder why Jesus had not chosen His devoted brother James, but both she and her youngest son had enough humility and trust to believe that there must be a pure and wise reason for His omission. The group was amazing. They worshipped and talked, and laughed together. They cooked fish on open fires on the shingle beach and they took early morning swims in the cold water of the lake. The insight that Jesus had into the meaning of scripture was astonishing and they sat at His feet like children and listened to His teaching. They sang psalms together, often convulsing with laughter at some of the painful disharmonies. Then they were on the move again.

The group, growing in number, travelled south down the western coast until they came to Magdala, a thriving agricultural and fishing town, situated at the junction of the road coming north from Tiberias and the Via Maris coming from the lower Galilee. West of the city, overlooked by Mount Arbel which rose 1,300 feet above the lake, was the Plain of Gennesaret and it was in this magnificent and picturesque setting that the people flocked in their thousands to hear Jesus and to see the miracles that He did. It was also here that another young woman called Mary first met the Saviour. Mary, the mother of Jesus, watched her as she pushed through the crowd and fell at the feet of her son. She was nicely dressed in clothes that showed her to be from a comfortable background, but she looked troubled. Her striking beauty was enhanced by her unusual long, red hair but her eyes were wild and full of fear, her arms and shoulders shaking with trauma. Her mind was a whirl of confusion, indecision, and torment. Sometimes the voices in her head almost drove her to suicide, a veritable flow of commands and counter-commands which gave her no peace. She was trapped in a world of mental and spiritual chaos from which there seemed no escape. She was in prison. She didn't know how she got there and she didn't know how to get out. As a result of her problems she was rejected by all and sundry, regarded as a neurotic nuisance, and spent much of her time walking and weeping in lonely places around Magdala. Then she heard about the man from Nazareth who was doing miracles in towns and cities all around the Galilee and hope rose in her heart. She was about to travel north to find Him when, miraculously it seemed to her, she heard that He was preaching on the plain just outside the city. Now she knelt imploringly at the feet of the Christ.

Mary continued to watch as she raised her tormented eyes to the eyes of Jesus.

"Master," she pleaded, "help me please, for I am tormented day and night. I have tried so hard and I have prayed to God, but I receive no help. Sometimes I cannot help myself and I take a knife and cut my arms. I don't want to die, but the voices in my head tell me to plunge the knife into my breast. I am afraid that I am going to do it. My days are as bad as the nightmares which invade my sleep. Please help me, Master, for I am told that you set such captives free."

Mary watched as Jesus placed His hand upon the forehead of the weeping woman. She drew closer, quietly praying for a miracle for this needy soul. She could just make out the words which came from the lips of Jesus. He did not raise His voice, but spoke in a tone of restrained aggression. He spoke as one would speak to an enemy, but with an attitude of total authority. She could not clearly hear His words, but He was obviously commanding some unseen intelligent force to leave the woman. The command was followed by another and then another. Seven times He spoke and seven times the woman shuddered from head to foot, until she lay prostrate and unconscious at His feet. He looked across at His mother for help and, as she moved to kneel at the side of the motionless form, He moved away to lay his hand upon a man who was blind.

Mary gently cushioned the young woman's head on her knees. She slept for several minutes, at rest in the morning sunshine. The light glistened on the grassy slopes of Mount Arbel, enhanced by the azure of a cloudless sky, and all was perfect peace. The girl opened her eyes. The fear was gone from those gateways to a now peaceful soul. Large green eyes floated in tears of unutterable joy. Her mind

was like the lake after a storm, perfectly still, no voices, no confusion. She did not move. Whoever this woman was who cradled her in her arms, she knew she was a friend. She felt at one with her, as though she had known her all her life.
"What is your name?" she asked the older woman.
"My name is Mary," came the gentle reply. The girl smiled, still resting where she was.
"Mine too," she said. "They call me Mary of Magdala, or just Mary Magdalene. Is your name just Mary?"
"They call me Mary, mother of Jesus," she replied.
The girl sat up suddenly. "You are His mother? Are you really His mother? I am sorry I should not have been so familiar with you." She began to get to her feet. Mary gently took her hand. "Why ever not?" she said. "I am only His mother, just an ordinary woman from Nazareth. I just try and help with the work, cooking meals and helping out where I can."

The two Marys stood facing each other on the Plain of Gennesaret, holding hands like they must never be parted. Salome saw her sister speaking with the stranger and approached them to say hello. Mary introduced the one to the other. It all seemed so inconsequential, so natural, so insignificant, but Jesus glanced across from a short distance away and saw the three women in a fond embrace. He smiled. Heaven smiled. This trio of women was no accident. Their meeting was foreknown from before time began. They were destined to serve as one in the cause of Christ. They would form the foundation support group for the ministry of Jesus. They would pray together, serve together, and with perfect unity love the Son of God through every torturous step of the road He was to walk.

By many people across the generations Mary Magdalene has been maligned and defamed without foundation. She has been charged with spending her early years in prostitution and blasphemously accused of becoming the lover of Jesus and the mother of children whom He never had. To Mary the mother of Jesus she was the dearest, most loyal and trusted friend. She joined the group, sharing the chores with her two new friends, putting her own money into buying provisions and paying expenses, and she did it all with a mind at perfect peace, devoted for ever to the service of the One who had opened the doors of her prison.

CHAPTER TWENTY

Salome's beloved Zebedee died peacefully in his sleep three months before she and Mary visited their nephew John in his prison at the Machaeus fortress in Parea. The widowed sisters then became inseparable. Together with Mary Magdalene they accompanied Jesus on most of His travels throughout Israel. Behind the scenes these three women were as important to God's plan as the trio of men, Peter, James and John, who were the inner circle of the apostolic band. Mary made occasional visits back to her home in Nazareth where she continued to support and love Joseph's children as her own, and Salome got to see home whenever the party returned to Capernaum, but Mary Magdalene never returned to Magdala; it had too many bad memories and there was nothing there for her anyway. The women were content to go wherever their Lord went. They considered it an immense privilege to serve Him with all their hearts. Mary the mother of Jesus was shaken when she discovered that her much-loved nephew, John the Baptist, was so cruelly murdered while she and her sister were walking away from Machaeus on the night of Herod's birthday, but she was so pleased that she was able to take him the message from Jesus which had so lifted his spirit. At least he had died in faith and in a mood of victory.

They were happy days. The work was hard and crowds followed them wherever they went. They never had a moment for themselves because people brought their sick to Jesus from dawn until evening on a daily basis. Mothers brought their children and husbands carried crippled wives on their shoulders. They brought the blind and the deaf and the diseased. Lepers stood back and cried for help from a distance. Mary wept with joy as these poor people went away whole. Surely there could be no greater joy than giving hope to the hopeless and help to the helpless. She often made her bed under the Galilean night sky and her eyes scanned the myriads of twinkling stars and she wondered about the mysterious previous life her son must have had somewhere beyond that dome of night lights.

She was troubled however. The last thirty years had seen economic decline in Israel. Since the death of Herod and the end of his vast building programmes, unemployment had soared and economic and political unrest was rampant. Everything was blamed on the hated Roman occupation. The people looked for a deliverer and Messianic talk was everywhere. Although Mary knew that their Messiah walked amongst them, she also knew that He did not fit the Jewish stereotype. He was in fact a source of annoyance to the authorities. He insulted the influential religious leaders, was outspoken in His condemnation of their hypocrisy and they knew that He was likely to bring the heavy hand of Rome down on them if they failed to control internal dissension. If anything Jesus was becoming too well known, too popular amongst the people for the liking of His enemies.

Then there occurred the amazing incident at Bethany. A man by the name of Lazarus lived there with his two sisters, Martha and Mary. They had on numerous occasions shown wonderful hospitality to Jesus and His followers and had become close friends. Then Lazarus fell very sick and by the time Jesus answered the call to help him he was dead. When Jesus and the group finally arrived they found that Lazarus had been dead and buried for four days. Mary then witnessed the most amazing miracle she could ever have imagined. In fulfilment of the vision she had seen at the burial cave of her husband fifteen years before, she watched as Jesus instructed that the stone be rolled away from the burial cave and with a loud voice He commanded the dead man to come forth. She saw with her own eyes the shrouded body shuffle from the tomb and, when loosed from the grave clothes, kneel in worship at the feet of Jesus. The miracle was witnessed by a number of influential people and the news of this sensation spread like a wild fire. Mary instinctively knew that this would cause a rage of jealousy amongst the religious leaders. The danger to her son had now increased one hundred fold. The smouldering fire of hatred against Jesus was turning into a raging inferno. The chief priests and Pharisees held council in Jerusalem. They feared a Roman backlash and ordered the arrest of Jesus should he appear in the city. It was now their avowed intent to have Him put to death. The public loved Him because He healed their sick and ministered to their needs, but Mary knew that the people were fickle and selfish and could turn in a moment. How she missed Joseph! How she would have loved to have shared with him her fears, asked his advice and rested her head on his strong shoulder. She knew that it was futile to offer her counsel to Jesus, not that He was above listening to His mother, but she knew He was now taking all his directions from His Father above. As a mother she wanted to stop Him going any further down the road He was on, but as a servant of God, in touch with the divine purposes, she knew that she could not and must not interfere. All she could do was stay close and try and be there for Him when the storm broke. It came as a great relief to her that at that time Jesus withdrew from public scrutiny and chose to live quietly in the city of Ephraim on the edge of the wilderness, although she guessed that it was more to do with timing than a permanent arrangement.

Her guess was proved correct when she discovered that He was planning to go to Jerusalem for the Feast of Passover. It was a suicidal move and all His friends, without exception, pleaded with Him not to go. There was no little tension amongst them. Mary was worried sick and the conversations she overheard between the disciples brought her no comfort.
"They are waiting for us," she heard Peter say. "They have actually issued a warrant for Jesus to be arrested."
"It's no good," said another. "He's made His mind up to go. I don't understand Him sometimes. You would think He wanted to be arrested."
Thomas was the most cutting, suggesting with cynical resignation, "We might as well all go and die with Him."
Mary felt the loneliness of her son. She sensed that He was being guided to Jerusalem by His Father and that He was fully aware of what awaited Him. He needed their support, not their criticism. She found it more difficult than all of them, but she knew that she must have faith. It was essential to trust, because heavy clouds of a coming storm were gathering in her mind and she knew that if she looked into the clouds she would see the face of the dragon. She also felt alone, because nobody understood as much

as she did. She had known this day would come in some form or another from the time this man had occupied her womb. Although Salome and her friend Mary, and another Mary, the wife of Cleopas, were the closest people in the world to her, they were like the men, still caught up in the traditional view of the kingly role of the Messiah.

Their view was fuelled once more by the scenes that greeted them as they approached the city. The people were still tingling with the excitement that permeated Jerusalem in the wake of the resurrection of Lazarus. Everybody wanted to see Jesus, and once the news began to circulate that He and his followers were approaching the town from the small community of Bethphage the crowds began to gather at the gate. Jesus had spent the night in Bethany with Lazarus and his sisters and was now descending the Mount of Olives to the Kidron Valley, to enter Jerusalem through the Eastern Gate which gave access directly to the Court of the Temple. The numbers grew until thousands lined the road into the city. Jesus was riding on a donkey, and, as He approached, the people began to sing His praise. They hailed Him as the Messiah. Their king had arrived to save them from the oppressor. The people engaged in a frenzy of excitement and emotion, tearing branches down from the palm trees, waving them triumphantly in the air and disrobing to lay their outer garments as a carpet before the feet of the ass. The disciples were smiling broadly. Perhaps they were wrong. Maybe it was right after all for them to come to Jerusalem. Surely the authorities would not dare to arrest Jesus in the face of such united support from the people.

Philip called across to Mary Magdalene. "This is amazing," he shouted. "Where's Mary?"
She shouted her reply. "She was here a few minutes ago. Oh, there she is, look, over there!"
Philip turned and called to Mary to join them. Then he saw her face. Her features were scourged with despair. An expression of deepest woe furrowed her suffering face. Tears were streaming down her haggard countenance, not tears of joy, but each tear drop an expression of the agony she felt. She took no pleasure in these emotional moments. She saw beyond the transient mood of the people. She knew that this was the last excuse His enemies needed. They would feel that they must halt this wave of dangerous popularity without delay. She heard the chorus of hosannas that filled the morning air, but they grew distorted in her ears. They gambled with the life of her beloved son. Their reckless euphoria was leading Him where she did not want Him to go. She looked up towards the Golden Gate and it became a gateway to death. A dark and bloody scene of sacrifice lay beyond the threshold of the Temple. She felt dizzy. Nausea surged. The ground moved under her feet. The sky spun and she felt herself falling. Then her face was buried in the coarse grass at the road side and she could hear the distant chorus of an angry crowd. The mob was screaming, "Crucify Him! Crucify Him! Crucify Him!"

CHAPTER TWENTY ONE

Mary usually enjoyed her visits to Bethany. Martha and Mary were very hospitable and Lazarus displayed a genuine affection for the mother of his Lord. It became home from home, a place of relaxation and recuperation in a stressful life. This time, however, things were different. The whole community was animated in the aftermath of the resurrection of Lazarus. Every day people came to gaze in wonderment at a man who had been dead for four days and returned to tell the story. Mary was not critical of them especially when she found herself staring at him herself, wanting to ask him if he could remember anything of the four days he was gone and what it felt like when he heard the distant voice of authority commanding him to live again, but the fact was that Bethany was no longer the peaceful safe haven she had come to love and appreciate. In addition to this, Mary was suffering under a cloud of anxiety concerning the obvious danger that Jesus was in. She was told that His triumphant entry into Jerusalem ended in a demonstration of indignation in the Court of the Temple which could be construed to indicate that he was deliberately provoking His enemies. There was a long standing corruption racket operating in the Temple, with extortionate prices being charged for the animals available for purchase for sacrifice use. Pilgrims obviously found it easier to buy what they needed at the Temple rather than herd their animals from a distance, but the merchants were in collusion with the Temple hierarchy who were being paid corruption money for promoting the business to the people. The scam also boosted the Temple taxes. Following her collapse as Jesus entered Jerusalem Mary was taken back to Bethany, but was horrified to hear later that day that Jesus had stormed into the Temple with a display of violence of which she would not have thought Him capable. He actually made a whip and drove the animals from what He announced with fiery passion was His Father's house. He threw the tables of the moneychangers over and the Temple court was evidently turned into a scene of mayhem, with money and feathers swirling in the air, animals scurrying and running amok and angry screaming men cursing Jesus. She wanted to go to Him, to ask Him why He was doing this, to reassure herself that He was following His Father's directions, but Martha pleaded with her not to go.

"He knows what He's doing Mary. He is so wise and listens always to His Father. I believe that He never does or says anything that does not come from His Father. Whatever is happening at the moment you must trust God. Please don't go and put yourself in danger because that will only put Jesus under even more pressure."

Mary knew her friend's council was good, so she put down her best motherly instincts and tried to relax. It was with some relief that she heard that Jesus was now quite calm and was giving himself to teaching in the Temple. Although the crowds continued to seek Him out, everything seemed to be much more peaceful. Jerusalem was busy preparing for the celebration of the Feast of Passover.

The news of His arrest came as a massive shock. The days of quiet had lulled Mary into a sense of false security, but the peace was the precursor to turmoil, the lull before the storm. News reached her in the early hours of the morning. Martha woke her with a shake of her shoulder and informed her that a young man by the name of Mark had run all the way from the city and was saying that Jesus had been arrested. She dressed with urgency and questioned the young man carefully about the events of the night. Jesus was evidently praying with Peter, James, and John in a garden on the Mount of Olives when one of His twelve apostles, Judas Iscariot, traitorously led a group of Temple police sent by Caiaphas the high priest to apprehend Him. The last Mark saw of Him He was being led down the slope towards the Kidron Valley. They had tied His arms behind His back and were leading Him like an animal with a rope tied around his neck.

Mary reacted with remarkable composure. There was no display of panic, no tears. A strange peace settled over her spirit. Then she asked a question which she almost feared to verbalise.

"Who was with Him? Did anybody go with Him?"

Mark lowered his eyes. His hands were trembling slightly.

"No Mary. Everybody ran away. Peter tried to fight them off to begin with, but Jesus told Him to put his sword away. After that I don't know what happened to everybody, but no, nobody went with Him. I'm sorry Mary; I was just watching from a distance and I didn't know what to do. I was scared."

"I must go to Him." Mary addressed the words to Martha, standing as she spoke.

"Please don't try and stop me! I will go back with Mark and try to help. He is my son, Martha. He needs me."

Martha wanted to prevent her but she knew it was pointless to try. Whatever the peril for her own life Mary had set her will to go to Jerusalem.

Clouds were drifting hastily across a watery moon, touching the dark streets of Jerusalem with occasional eerie illumination, as Mary, on the arm of the teenage Mark, made her way towards the house of Caiaphas the high priest. The area was deserted, except for the lone figure of a man, apparently drunk, who was lurching towards them. His head was bent forwards, his shoulders hunched, his beard buried in his chest. As he drew closer she observed that his whole body was heaving with sobs. Some deep anguish was tearing the heart out of the stranger. In his distraction he almost collided with them, but as he stepped aside their eyes met. They both shuddered to a halt, recognition freezing them in the moment.

"Peter, is it you? What is wrong? What have they done?" She was gripping his arm, a look of terrible fear in her eyes.

"Mary, it is not what they have done, it is what I have done. I have betrayed my Lord. Mary I have done a terrible thing. They accused me of being with Him and I denied it. I was scared. In my cowardice I told them that I had never seen Him before. Three times I did it. I even took an oath that I didn't know Him. He heard me, Mary. He looked at me. He had such pain and sadness in His eyes. I failed Him."

"What have they done to Him Peter? Where is He now?"

"They accused Him of blasphemy. They treated Him badly Mary. They mocked Him. They put a blindfold over His eyes and then punched Him in the face. They were laughing and asking Him to prophesy which one of them had hit Him. I think that they are now taking Him to Pilate for judgement. I think they want to kill Him. I left him Mary. I betrayed my best friend in the whole world."

"Is nobody with Him Peter? Did they all leave Him?"

"John's in there. He knows the high priest, but he won't be allowed to stay with Him when they go to Pilate."

Peter's face was convoluted with grief. Mary, ever a woman of compassion, reached her hand out to his, but he gently pushed it away and continued his bereft journey to nowhere, the sound of his weeping following in his wake.

Mary knocked loudly on the door of the house of Caiaphas and demanded access from the guard who came to answer it. He was tired and grumpy.

"Go away, woman!" he snarled.

"But the man you have is my S…" The door slammed in her face. She turned to follow Peter, but he was gone, lost in the shadows of the night, and lost in the dreadful darkness of his own soul. She shivered in the cold as she took Mark's arm.

"Take me to the judgment hall of Pilate."

CHAPTER TWENTY TWO

Pilate's judgment hall was part of his palace in the huge Antonia Fortress which was built in 35 BC by Herod the Great to protect the Temple Mount. He named it after his friend Mark Antony. Each corner of the magnificent building sported a tower, three of them 75ft tall, and the fourth, the north-western tower, was a full 115ft. Stairs connected the Antonia Fortress to the Temple area. It was a military fortification serving as the headquarters and barracks for Roman soldiers as well as a palace for the Roman procurator. The eastern wall overlooked the Pool of Bethesda and the Kidron valley whilst the southern wall overlooked the whole of the Temple area. It was to this impressive place of judgment that Jesus was brought to answer before Pontius Pilate. The Jewish counsel in the house of Caiaphas had basically already sentenced Him to death, but, as they were not allowed to carry out the sentence themselves, it needed to be ratified and executed by the Roman authorities.

It was still dark over Temple Mount as Mary mingled with the chattering crowds that were speedily amassing in the fortress courtyard. News of the arrest of Jesus had amazingly already reached the staff that lived within the precincts of Antonia and, hungry for excitement and sensationalism, they left their beds and rushed out to witness the fate of the famous Jesus of Nazareth. The atmosphere was surreal as the ghostly figures of the pressing crowd moved like a slow moving sea in the light of innumerable flaming torches. It was strange for Mary to hear the gossip of the people, some saying good things about her son, others saying bad things, and others, the plainly ridiculous. She felt alone and isolated in the milling throng. Her stomach was knotted with emotional pain and she felt sick and weak with worry and apprehension. She desperately wanted to contact Jesus that she might offer Him words of comfort and support, but He was nowhere to be seen.

The actual judgment hall was a no-go area for religious Jews, especially at a time like this. The Feast of Passover was upon them and this was no time to risk becoming ceremonially unclean by entering a Roman court as this would exclude them from taking part in the feast. It is ever an enigma how religion can fastidiously adhere to ritual perfection whilst being the perpetrator of extreme and callous evil. So Jesus faced Pilate and His Roman spectators inside the judgment hall whilst His accusers and the people, who were fast turning into an unruly mob, waited in the courtyard. This meant that Mary, still leaning on the arm of the young man Mark, found herself waiting helplessly for the result of a scene which was being played out beyond her view or control. Justice mattered nothing to the majority of these people. They were part of this for the theatre, not because they cared or didn't care. They had no idea as they enjoyed the unfolding spectacle of the unexpected event that standing amongst them was a mother with a breaking heart.

After what seemed like an eternity Pilate emerged to question the priests who were both the perpetrators of the chaos and the reason why he had been called so early from his bed. He wanted to know what the details of the charges were and by his curt manner and aggressive tone he was obviously far from convinced that they were legitimate. The priests were agitated. They insisted that they would not have gone to the trouble of bringing Jesus to him if he were not guilty. All they required from Pilate was his authorisation of the death penalty and they were anxious to proceed with their plans as soon as possible. Pilate, however, appeared troubled. Whatever the exchange between the judge and the accused had been within the secret confines of the judgement hall something had made an impression on this normally hard-hearted Roman. He was to be no pushover and he had no intention of being dragged from his bed to simply be used as a means to an end by a group of jealous, religious, Jewish bigots.

"Take Him and judge Him according to your own law," he snapped.

"We already have! He is worthy of death! But only you can authorise this."

The Jews knew that they would not prevail if it appeared that there were only religious reasons for their hatred of Jesus so they made accusation that Jesus was guilty of insurrection against Rome, saying that He claimed to be the rightful king of the Jews. They also bore false witness that He was forbidding the people to pay tribute to Caesar. The debate continued and eventually, much to the delight of the people, Pilate commanded that Jesus be brought out briefly before the crowd to answer certain questions. Mary wanted him to know that she was there. He was so close and yet so unreachable. She wanted to shout out, "I love you," but wisdom restrained her.

Then they were inside again and the crowd waited. After some time Pilate reappeared looking tired and worried and not a little angry. He called for silence and then with a cold and steely glare at the priestly hypocrites before him he announced, "I find in Him no fault at all." Mary burst into tears of relief, but the priests were furious. They fearlessly denounced Pontius Pilate and accused him of betraying Rome and failing Caesar himself. The Procurator found himself trapped between the voice of his conscience and his fear of what these people could stir up against him. The last thing he wanted was a riot in Jerusalem or problems with his superiors. Then it occurred to him that if the accused was from Galilee he could perhaps avoid the final responsibility of this whole matter by referring it to Herod Antipas, the tetrarch of Galilee, and allowing him to deal with it. He subsequently issued the necessary command and Jesus was marched away, flanked by soldiers of Rome, to give an account before the man who had beheaded His cousin John.

It was not yet 5a.m. and Mary sat on a low stone wall within the fortress grounds as the crowd thinned. Some pursued the soldiers thinking they might gain access to Herod's palace, others returned to their quarters, whilst many more just gathered in groups talking about the events of the night and speculating as to their outcome. Mary sat with her head in her hands and prayed for her son and for herself. She tried to take hope from Pilate's unwillingness to act against Jesus but deep within she knew that this was it. The prophets of old were beginning to weep at the fulfilment of their dark utterances concerning the Messiah.

They were back within the hour and so was the crowd, drawn by an unannounced macabre knowledge that blood was to be spilt. Herod had enjoyed a little sport in mocking Jesus but returned him to Pilate for final judgment. There were too many variables in this very public case for Herod to put his neck in the noose. Pilate was not pleased.

"I have told you that after careful examination I find no fault in this man. Obviously Herod could find no cause of death either, so my decision is made. I will punish Him and then release Him."

Cajoled by the priests sections of the growing crowd began chanting, "Away with Him! Kill Him! Crucify Him! Crucify Him!"

Pilate's back was to the wall. This entire situation was getting out of hand and he was in danger of being made to look a fool. Then he had another idea. The Jews had a baroque convention at their Feast of Passover which allowed for the freeing of a convicted felon by the popular choice of the people. He decided to offer them the opportunity of giving freedom to a convicted criminal and murderer by the name of Barabbas or the release of Jesus of Nazareth, believing that the thought of loosing onto the streets of Jerusalem a known cut-throat and bandit would swing it in favour of the Nazarene. He was wrong. The crowd were now thirsty for the blood of the Nazarene. The cry went up with more fervour than ever, "Release Barabbas! Give us Barabbas!"

"But what about Jesus?"

"Crucify Him! Crucify Him."

Mary cringed at the cruelty of the mob. The words of the prophet now filled her mind.

"He was taken from prison and from judgment: and who shall declare His generation, for He was cut off out of the land of the living?"

She knew that there was no going back from this. She knew that as Pilate took Jesus back into the court to have Him scourged as a last desperate effort to gain the sympathy of the people that it would make no difference. These events were already written in stone. This was why her beloved Son was born. The purpose of her life was to bring Him to this day. The predictive words of the psalmist were now fulfilled, "Lo, I come: in the volume of the book it is written of me, I come to do Thy will O God." This bizarre and unjust scenario was planned from the beginning of time for the redemption of mankind. God was in Christ reconciling the world to Himself through the sacrifice of the one true Passover Lamb.

She wept quietly as she waited, aware that her son was being beaten with thirty-nine stripes, but unaware of the unadulterated brutality and hatred which inspired each vicious lash. The first rays of the morning sun were lighting the scene as He emerged. They had dressed Him in a scarlet robe and a huge ring of thorns was rammed into His head. His eyes were blinded with the flow of blood and He was obviously finding it difficult to walk. Pilate signalled to the guard who roughly pulled the robe from the body of the Saviour. She gasped with horror as she saw the bloody mass of open flesh that her son had been reduced to. He was now naked except for a rag tied around His waist. His face was a mass of bruises and cuts. They had torn out His beard and with it the skin of His face. His torso was a bleeding mass of open wounds.

The flagellum, a whip made of braided leather thongs of different lengths in which small iron balls and slithers of sheep's bone were tied at intervals, had cut through His skin and tissue and through into His skeletal muscles. Long strands of blood-oozing flesh were hanging from His pain-shocked body. He was weakened by the severe blood loss and barely able to stand. He was also suffering the effects of sleep deprivation, hunger and extreme thirst. She yearned to take His broken body in her arms, bathe His wounds, carry him away from this living hell and tell Him how much she loved Him, but she could not. She cried out at the top of her voice, "I'm here Jesus, I'm here!" but her voice was drowned out by the rising chorus of "Crucify Him! Crucify Him! Crucify Him!" She pushed her way fearlessly through the howling mob, inching her way closer to her son, all the time shouting His name. His blood veiled eyes were scanning the crowd looking for her, but He could not find her and her voice was lost in the wind of noise. It was her reckless intention to fight her way to His side, to declare who she was, to die with him if necessary. She wanted to die with Him. She wanted to share His pain. He was flesh of her flesh, and if His flesh was suffering she wanted hers to feel it also. She was within yards of reaching her goal when her arms were seized by two pairs of hands on each side. She swung round. On her right was her friend, Mary Magdalene, and on her left, her sister Salome.

"Mary, wait! They will kill you!"

"I want them to kill me. I want to die with Him. Let me go. I want to go to Him."

She was sobbing now, her body convulsed with imprudent sorrow. She tried to free her arms from the restraints of her friends.

"But Mary, He would not want that. It will only add to His suffering if they hurt you. You must be strong for Him now. He needs to know that you are safe. We will stay together and, whatever happens, we will all be there for Him."

Mary knew that her sister was right and the last thing she wanted was to make things worse for Jesus. She resigned her body to what now became the supporting arms of the two women and they stood together in silent horror as the scene played out before them.

Pilate signalled to be heard and an uneasy silence settled over the crowd. A servant appeared with a bowl of water and a towel. The Jews gasped as the Roman Procurator adopted a Jewish custom as a final attempt to save an innocent life. He ceremonially washed his hands whilst declaring in a voice lifted up with all the authority he could muster,

"I am innocent of the blood of this righteous man. See to it yourselves."

A priest called back defiantly, "His blood be upon us and upon our children! Crucify him!"

"That's right," said another. "We want him crucified!"

Then the chorus began again, a united rising cacophony of evil music, rising to a crescendo of deafening hatred. "Crucify him! Crucify him! Crucify him!"

Pilate knew that he had lost his fight. He dried his hands, turned to his centurion, and inclined his head towards the prisoner. His voice was subdued, resigned.

"Crucify him!"

He turned to leave as the soldiers closed in on the Son of God. As he did so his eyes settled on a woman in the crowd. Her eyes were desperate, pleading, full of love, and tears were streaming down her weary face. A look of indescribable agony haunted her features and her hands and arms were open as a woman holds her arms to a falling child. He instinctively knew that it was His mother. For a moment their eyes were linked and sorrow met pity, before pity turned away.

CHAPTER TWENTY THREE

It was a common sight to see a troop of Roman soldiers descending the steps from the Antonia Fortress to head north towards the Fish Gate. Every day criminals, thieves, and murderers were led that way to the place of execution outside the city walls. To the casual onlooker the group escorting Jesus was no different from any other. He was just another transgressor on his way to deservedly pay for his crimes. For Mary it was the day she had dreaded since she was sixteen years old. Here came the sword to pierce her soul. Her mind was full of the scriptures she had known from her youth …. "He was numbered with the transgressors ….. He was led as a lamb to the slaughter …..He made his grave with the wicked ….. He is despised and rejected of men."

She watched her son's every step with longing. She wanted so much to share His burden. The authorities had torn the red robe of mockery from His wounded back and put on Him His own woven outer garment. They were compelling Him to carry the cross on which He was going to die but He was too weak and the merciless flogging He had received had inflicted appalling open wounds on His back. These lacerations together with the ensuing blood loss made it impossible for Him to carry the load. He managed to stumble a few yards, but Mary could see that He was about to fall under its weight. She impulsively decided to help Him, moving with such speed that it took her companions totally by surprise. She broke rank and dashed between the soldiers to the side of her collapsing Son, throwing her weight under the rough timber to lift it clear of His shoulders, but she was already too late. Jesus had already started to fall and her efforts served only to unbalance the cross. They fell together, mother and son, trapped between the heavy timber and the dry hard path beneath them. For an instant they were face to face. She gazed into his bloodshot eyes and poured into them her unutterable love. His marred and broken visage attempted the faintest of smiles and His eyes spoke into her soul.

"All will be well mother. This is why I came. You bore me in your womb and suckled me at your breast in order that I might do this today. You knew this day would come. I am the Passover Lamb, sacrificed for the salvation of the world."

It was a silent exchange between two souls made one. It lasted for just seconds, but seemed an eternity of union, before rough hands grabbed the loose collar of her robe and threw her backwards into the road. A soldier hauled Jesus to His feet whilst another accosted a passer by, a man by the name of Simon, who became the unwilling carrier of the cross of Jesus.

So it was that the one known as "The Carpenter's Son" came to a place called Golgotha, and so it was that a mother of fifty years of age watched the agonising death of her firstborn son. Never in the throes of her worst nightmares had she previewed or imagined the horror of those hours. She cringed as they removed His robe and exposed his nakedness. His flesh was a mass of bleeding wounds and she was incredulous that He could still be alive after such a beating. She wondered where her son James was. Surely he could not have forsaken the brother he loved so much in his hour of greatest need? She needed James now, but he was nowhere to be seen. Only her female friends stood at her side supporting her, one on each side, united in their funereal grief.

She watch helplessly as they stretched her willing son onto the cross as it lay on the ground and fastened Him to it with huge nails which they hammered through His hands and feet. He did not cry out. It was as though the pain was just absorbed into the burning experience of torture which already consumed His flesh. She turned away as they raised the gibbet high and dropped it into its socket, and when she looked back she saw that the jolt had disjointed some of His bones and they had broken through His torn flesh and were protruding through His skin. She felt a wave of nausea sweep over her and thought that she would faint. Strong hands took hold of her shoulders from behind and the voice of her sister's son John spoke to comfort her.
"Mary," he said. "I know this is hard for you but we must be strong. This suffering will pass and then we will see the reason for it all."
He pulled her head gently to his chest. "Here, rest your weight against me and we will pray for Him together."

It was 9a.m. and the spring sunshine was pleasantly warm. Jesus was groaning with pain, vainly attempting to raise His torso to get air into His lungs. Blood was dripping slowly from His bruised feet. The soldiers and priests were not content with the torment provided by the crucifixion, but sought to add to His affliction with much mockery and verbal abuse. There were two others being executed with Jesus, but their personal agony did not prevent them joining in the slandering of the Saviour. Mary scanned the faces of the crowd around the cross to see if she could see Peter anywhere. She hoped that Jesus had not noticed his absence. She checked a feeling of indignance towards the men whom Jesus had trusted, men who were now showing a cowardice and self-pity in the face of affliction which beggared belief. She thought how easy it is to make statements of commitment when all is well, only to fail miserably when put to the test. She desired to gently soothe her son's open wounds. She yearned to wash away His pain with the tears of her love. She wanted to hide the shame of His nakedness. She wanted to touch His lacerated feet. Meanwhile a group of soldiers were casting lots for who would inherit the woven garment of their victim.

Then He spoke. His glazed eyes were looking with tender pity upon His persecutors but his words were words of prayer to His Father.
"Father, forgive them, for they not what they do."
Mary stood rigid with astonishment. She was overwhelmed with the wonder of true forgiveness, because it was obvious that He sincerely wanted His Father to forgive these people. This was not a prayer said for effect; He was actually asking that this dreadful crime would not be accounted to these men. He wanted them to be excused. The dying thief to his right heard His words and scornfully suggested that if Jesus was who He claimed to be He might like to save them all from their fate, but he was immediately rebuked by his fellow criminal.
"Dost not thou fear God, seeing thou art in the same condemnation? And we indeed justly; for we receive the due rewards of our deeds: but this man hath done nothing amiss."

He turned his eyes to those of Jesus and pleaded, "Lord, remember me when thou comest into Thy kingdom."
Jesus paused for a moment and replied, "Verily I say unto thee, Today shalt thou be with Me in paradise."

The two Marys and Salome were joined in their sorrowful vigil by the other Mary, wife of Cleopas, and stood with John to wait the inevitable death of their loved one. The women openly wept. John also wanted to weep, but controlled his emotions for the sake of the others.
Jesus addressed His mother in the gentlest of tones.
"Woman, behold thy son," He said.
Mary looked into His eyes a little hurt that He did not call her "mother" but understanding that the man who bled before her was dying, not as the son of Mary, but as the Son of God. Of course she wanted him to say "mother" but she knew that as the "Passover Lamb" He could not. He had removed himself from every human relationship in order that He might fulfil His father's plan. She also recognised that He was not asking her to look at Him, but at the beloved disciple who stood at her side. Jesus dearly loved His young cousin, John, who was only just twenty years of age and yet the only one of His disciples brave enough to associate himself with His cross. She looked up into the face of John as Jesus spoke to His friend,
"Behold thy mother!"
Jesus was asking John to take care of His mother. Mary was immediately conscious that her widowed sister Salome needed the help of her son and would need it more in future days. She turned to search her sister for her reaction, but there was no sign of jealousy or resentment, nothing but love and support. She knew that Mary would be more in

need of help than herself. She bent and whispered in her sister's ear, "He will take good care of you, Mary. He's a good young man." The sisters embraced and wept in each other's arms.

For three hours they watched Him suffer. There were periods of silence when the only sound was of the heavy breathing of the dying men and the haunting cry of a lone vulture circling over the blood-drenched scene. The sun had risen to its zenith and it was unusually hot for springtime. The bloody sweat was stinging the eyes of Jesus and Mary could see it was becoming more difficult for Him to breathe. What shame, what agony, what undiluted hell was unleashed against her son! What evil had demanded such a price and what divine love had agreed to pay it? Then the atmosphere suddenly changed. The light appeared shrouded in a lowering mist and a strange chill ran through her aching body. She looked up into the heavens. The sun had disappeared behind dark, supernatural clouds. Layer upon layer of dark blankets clothed the heavens until the darkness was complete, as caliginous as a moonless night. Mary stepped forward and steadied herself against the blood-soaked upright of the cross as Jesus exhaled the most heart-rending cry of agony that has ever been heard by mortal man. It was a cry of astonished anguish, a question, which by the truth of its content was destined to receive no answer. The Son of God addressed his Father,
"My God, My God, why hast Thou forsaken Me?"
The silence could be felt, as though the words of Jesus were frantically searching the empty heavens for an absent God.

He was nowhere to be found. Heaven itself had closed the door on its beloved.

Mary rehearsed the words of the psalm which followed the quotation her son had just uttered.

"Why art Thou so far from helping me, and from the words of my roaring? ....I am a worm and no man; a reproach of men and despised of the people. All they that see me laugh me to scorn: they shoot out the lip, they shake the head, saying, He trusted on the Lord that he would deliver him: let him deliver him, seeing he delighted in him. But Thou art he that took me out of the womb ..." Mary's mind went back in an instant to the time that He had inhabited her womb. She saw a mental image of a sixteen year-old girl with hands resting tenderly upon her swollen belly.... "Thou didst make me hope when I was upon my mother's breasts." She relived for a moment the inexplicable warmth and beauty of her baby suckling hungrily at her breast. Then it was back to the man, the suffering dying man, swallowed in the blackness of the noontime night.

For three hours she strained her caring eyes to see Him in the heavy gloom. She sensed death, flanked by legions of demons, closing in on Mount Golgotha. Her legs and back were aching with the strain of the six hours of standing on the rough terrain, but she refused to sit, determined to fellowship with His sufferings in whatever way she could. Mary of Magdala wept continuously but uttered not a word.

It was approaching 3p.m. when He next spoke. He was close to death and His body was dehydrated. His breathing was intermittent and shallow. His voice was restricted by

His parched condition and His tongue was cleaving to the roof of His mouth.

"I thirst."

There was no limit to the cruelty of His persecutors. It would have cost them nothing to soothe His broken lips with a little water, but instead they soaked a sponge with vinegar and, spearing it on the end of a pole, pressed it against His mouth. Mary wanted to scream her protest. She wanted to wrest the pole from the hands of the soldier and use it against him. She was long past caring for her own safety. She wanted this wickedness to stop. He had done nothing to deserve any of this and the sense of injustice suddenly fuelled a fire of righteous indignation in her soul. She removed herself from the restraining arms of her friends and stepped towards her son's abuser. What she might have done and what consequences she would have suffered will never be known for it was then, providentially, that Jesus uttered His final words. They were spoken with an authority energised by the victory they announced. It was as though all His remaining resources of strength were summoned for this final announcement to the world. They were not the words of a man whose life was being taken but the words of a man who was laying down His life for the salvation of the world.

"It is finished!" was His cry followed by, "Father, into Thy hands I commend my spirit!"

Mary stopped in her impetuous mission. She stood alone for a moment on this desolate hill of death with her face uplifted to the heavens. She looked into the swirling clouds of darkness above her and saw there the face of the dragon. She had felt its vile presence for hours, gloating, laughing and mocking her sorrow. It was as though it felt its revenge for the birth in Bethlehem long ago was complete.

But the face of evil was not laughing now for the final words of Jesus brought with them a dread realisation to the dragon that what he thought was victory might be a terrible defeat. His obscene face was contorted with horror, his eyes shrinking with fear. The clouds were receding, sucking the monster into a vortex of judgment. Mary felt the ground beneath her feet trembling with the power of another world. She fell to her knees at the foot of the cross as the earth quaked and shuddered across Jerusalem. It was done! The price was paid in full! She placed her hands upon the feet of the dead man before her. She meant to say "My son, my son" but instead she found herself gazing at the blood on her hands and saying over and over again, "My Saviour, My Saviour, My Saviour!"

CHAPTER TWENTY FOUR

Salome tried to gently persuade her sister to leave the gory scene of death, but Mary would not, could not leave. The light had returned although the sun was already dipping into the west. The shadows cast by the three gruesome gallows were lengthening across the litter scattered scene, the only sound being the barely audible groans of the dying thieves. The spectators slowly dispersed until only the five comforters of Christ were left. Mary finally surrendered to her aching limbs and slumped exhausted to the ground. She gazed with agonised adoration upon the lifeless corpse of her son. A soldier wandered across to the man on the cross to the right of Jesus. The following day was a special Sabbath in the Passover celebrations and it was unlawful for anybody to be hanging on a cross on such a high day. It was the soldier's duty to ensure that the victims were dead and have their bodies removed before darkness fell. He slammed the shaft of his spear against the legs of the dying man. The bones broke with a sickening crack and his body slumped down and robbed him of the ability to breath. He was dead within a minute. The soldier then gazed up at Jesus, saw that He was already dead and passed on to break the legs of the second thief. Mary watched the soldier turn away. Their eyes met for a moment, his both cold and cruel, hers soft with sorrow and love. In that instant he instinctively knew who she was. This was the Nazarene's mother. He wanted to hurt her, to violate her love, to incite a reaction, so he swung round and with one vicious act plunged his spear into the side of her dead son. A stream of blood and water poured from the wounded side of Christ and exploded onto the ground. It splashed across the feet and legs of the soldier. He kicked the ground contemptuously and walked away without a backward glance.

A tall man approached Mary as though he knew her. He was, in fact, somewhat familiar to her. She thought that she had seen him amongst the people who sometimes followed Jesus from place to place listening to his teaching. He introduced himself.

"Mary, my name is Joseph. I am from the village of Arimathea and I am a believer and follower of your Son. I was here today as He was suffering and when He finally expired I took the liberty of going to Pilate and asking permission to remove His body from the cross. I don't want the soldiers to do it. I own a tomb in the garden just below this place and I have brought clean linen to wrap His body in. I would consider it an honour if you would allow me to tend your Son's body and lay Him in the tomb which I have prepared for my eventual decease."

Mary smiled her appreciation.

"Thank you, Joseph, you are very kind. I would very much appreciate you doing that for me."

Another man appeared as though from nowhere. His name was Nicodemus, another secret follower of Jesus, and the two of them, together with John, lifted the cross from its socket and lowered it carefully to the ground. They removed the emaciated form of Jesus from its bondage and wrapped it in the shroud which Joseph had brought. Joseph and Nicodemus then gently lifted the corpse and, followed by the small procession of mourners, walked the short distance down to the garden tomb. There they laid the body of the Messiah in the silence of the cave and there a mother kissed the shrouded face of her firstborn son and whispered her goodbyes.

The men rolled the stone across the opening to the tomb and Mary walked away. She wanted Joseph. She wanted to go home to Nazareth. She wanted to walk in and find her husband laughing at the bench with Jesus. She wanted to turn back the clock and have it all like it used to be. John took her hand, "Come on, mother," he smiled. "Let's go and eat."

It was 7p.m. when they arrived at John's house in Jerusalem and almost dark. A lone figure was lurking in the shadows as they approached, his cloak pulled up over his bowed head, his body language nervous and hesitant. It was Peter. He looked terrible. John spoke kindly to his friend, "Come inside Peter and have something to eat." Immediately Peter began to sob uncontrollably, his ample shoulders heaving with each convulsion of sorrow. He took Mary's arm. "Is He dead, Mary? Have I killed Him?"
"He is dead Peter," she replied, "But you did not kill Him. Nobody killed Him. He offered up His life as atonement for the sins of the world. You were a coward, my friend, and you deserted Him in his hour of need, but you did not kill Him."
They walked in silence up the steps into a nicely furnished room which was part of an above average dwelling in Jerusalem, and John trimmed the candles. The rest of the women had gone back to Bethany, so it was just the three of them who sat in the flickering lamplight and talked about the dreadful happenings of the day. Mary could

sense Peter's agony. He wanted to know what happened, but at the same time recoiled from hearing the truth. Her compassion wanted to help him, tell him he was forgiven, offer him reassurance for the future, but the spiritual woman knew that it was premature. He needed to get the message, to recover himself to a position from which he would never fall again. If he was to be the rock that Jesus said he was called to be, he must never again act the coward.

She found it difficult to go to sleep. The hellish memories of the day washed over her mind and robbed her of peace. She tried to pray but to no avail. She felt so alone, so utterly bereft. From the moment that she knew that she was pregnant thirty-four years before, she had lived and moved and worked for the precious son bequeathed to her care, and now He was gone, and with Him the very purpose of her life. She felt her life had ended. She had finished her course and there was nothing left for her to do. She just wanted to go and find her son, to be with him for a moment more, even if it meant trespassing beyond the gates of death. She felt guilty for wanting to die and then fell into a disturbed sleep. She dreamed that she was a girl in her twenties walking up her favourite hill in Nazareth with her young son. The sun was shining and Jesus was laughing and skipping ahead of her. She thought how much like her He was. She used to do the very same thing as a child. Suddenly heavy black clouds embraced the scene and a powerful wind swirled around the child, lifting Him into the air and sucking Him into the darkness. The happy look on His face twisted into fear and horror. His arms were reaching for His mother, but he was being pulled away. She tried to run towards Him but her legs would not move. She tried to call His name but no words would come. He screamed as He disappeared into the blackness. She woke, sobbing and wet with perspiration. Someone was banging on the door. She heard John pulling the bolts, then voices in the hallway. She dressed quickly and walked through into the adjoining room. Her son James was standing shamefacedly in the centre of the room.

CHAPTER TWENTY FIVE

Mary did not spare her son the sharp end of her tongue. She was saddened and indignant concerning what she regarded as a serious betrayal of brotherly love. If James was looking for maternal comfort he was seriously disappointed. She treated him with a coldness he had not experienced from her before.

"I cannot believe that a son of mine could be such a coward," she scolded. "You claimed to love Him and follow Him. You pledged yourself not just to your brother, but to your Messiah and Lord, but as soon as you felt danger for yourself you failed and deserted Him. When it came to it, James, you were only interested in saving your own skin. Your behaviour was reprehensible and I am ashamed of you!"

She turned away with tears of anger and sorrow in her eyes.

The apostles arrived one by one throughout the day, abashed and downcast with guilt. First was her nephew, James, the son of Salome, brother of John, one of the three whom Jesus chose to accompany Him into the garden of Gethsemane on the night of His betrayal. He suffered the same reception as James, the Lord's brother, receiving no mercy either from Mary or his brother, John. He was followed by Philip and Nathaniel, Thomas and Matthew and the others. It was a strained atmosphere to say the least, a strange ambient cocktail of bereavement, indignation, guilt and regret. After the initial forthright expressions of disapproval an uneasy silence reigned. Mary knew that they could not go back and undo their mistakes, but she wanted them to learn the lesson and be right for the future. She felt that Peter was probably the most repentant of them all. He acted as a servant towards her, waiting on her needs with sincere humility, not trying to placate her, but because he genuinely wanted to help and comfort her in her loss. She could feel his unfeigned care and concern as he busied himself around the house.

Rumours filtered through into the home. The Romans had evidently put their military seal on the tomb of Jesus and set a guard in case His followers tried to steal away the body and then later claim that He had been raised from the dead. The news lightened the atmosphere a little. It did seem slightly amusing that the Romans found it necessary to guard a corpse and, if they feared some kind of resurrection story, perhaps His followers should be thinking a little more positively. Later in the day they received the news that the traitor, Judas Iscariot, had killed himself. It was a gory tale, but the report was that after he had sold Jesus to the Jews he had returned to the priests in a fit of regret, thrown the pieces of silver at their feet and proceeded to hang himself from the branch of a tree. The branch broke under his weight and as his body hit the ground his belly split open and his innards burst out. The news was met with horrified silence for they all knew that there was not a huge difference between his act of betrayal and their own craven desertion of their friend. This account was quickly followed by another rumour that the Jewish authorities were planning to search out all the followers of Jesus with the intention of killing them all. They knew that the fact that today was a special Sabbath guaranteed their safety for the remainder of the day, but that tomorrow things could be very different. The evil tidings was probably a fabrication, but they were all scared, a fact which was underlined the next morning by a lack of volunteers offering to go out and buy some much needed food and drink. It was only when Mary, further grieved by their continuing cowardice, shamed them by offering to go herself that her son, James, and his namesake, the son of Zebedee, reluctantly volunteered and ventured out into the street.

They found Jerusalem unchanged. Commerce was flowing and people were going about their daily business as they always did. Children were playing happily in the streets. Trapped in their own world of sorrow and confusion and guilt the cousins felt that the whole scene was surreal, but the fact was that here in the street, amongst the bustling populace out doing their shopping for tomorrow's regular Sabbath, it was as though the last few days had never happened and nobody even gave them a second glance. They walked briskly into the market place and bought their provisions. Neither of them felt comfortable and they were anxious to get back to John's house as soon as possible.

When they returned they discovered a considerably brighter scene. Mary Magdalene and Mary the wife of Cleopas had arrived from Bethany and the women were chatting as though they hadn't seen each other for weeks. It was hard to realise that it was only forty-eight hours since Jesus had expired in such agony on the cross. At least people were communicating in the house and some of the strained atmosphere seemed to have lifted. The talk was mainly concerning Jesus and their future aspirations and desires. Mary was clinging to the belief that there was still something important in the somewhat obscure references that her Son had made regarding a resurrection. She entertained no doubt about Him being the promised Messiah, and if she was right, these present circumstances could not possibly be the end. Jesus must somehow appear again and fulfil the prophetic utterances of the ancients. She could see clearly how Jesus had lived out the scriptures regarding suffering, but surely He must now fulfil the predictions of the prophets regarding power and glory and kingship. The women tended to agree with Mary, but the men were sceptical. They adopted an attitude of resignation to the undoubted facts before them, acknowledging that they had been wrong in their misplaced expectations. The Romans were obviously still in control of Israel. Everything outside continued as it was and the man they thought was their deliverer was dead. The only reason they were together was that they were afraid to be anywhere else. As soon as the dust settled and the perceived danger was passed they would all go their separate ways, back to tax collecting or political activating, or back to fishing Lake Galilee which would also conveniently take them a safe distance away from this city of lost dreams.

The house was now crowded and the night was unseasonably warm. There were bodies everywhere and Mary spent another restless night alone with her memories, sometimes listening again to the words of the old man in the Temple as he gazed into the face of her new born son or watching her curly haired toddler rolling in the dirt outside her home at Bethlehem, sometimes standing at the funeral service of her beloved Joseph, but inevitably, whether asleep or awake, reliving the dark hell of Golgotha. She was relieved when the sky paled with the advent of another dawn.

It was a strange day. Although it was the Sabbath nobody seemed inclined to go to the Temple. A mixture of pathos and fear conspired to imprison them in the house, but there was more to it than that. Mary felt a deep sense of emptiness, almost like the Temple itself was now redundant, like an era had passed and the presence of the Lord was departed. She was not afraid to go out but felt no desire to attend the Sabbath service so instead she spent some time alone in prayer with her Heavenly Father, a time which brought a sense of peace and tranquillity to her heart. The words of the psalmist drifted through her mind, "The Lord is my rock, my fortress, and my deliverer." A little later the others heard her singing softly to herself as she prepared the Sabbath meal.

As the time reached 6p.m. at the end of the Sabbath a strange stillness settled over her spirit, a silence that was pregnant with a feeling of anticipation. It was now the first day of a new week and she inexplicably entertained a desire to visit the tomb of her son. She knew it would be foolish to set out so late in the day because it would necessitate returning in the darkness of late evening when danger lurked in the back streets of Jerusalem, but she determined to make the journey to the sacred garden at first light. Her sister, Salome, and Mary Magdalene, without any prompting from Mary, also expressed a desire to visit the tomb and anoint the body of Jesus. So the arrangement was made and as the first hint of light tinged the eastern sky, while it was still dark, the three women quietly dressed and slipped out of John's house into the street and headed for the Fish Gate.

CHAPTER TWENTY SIX

It was an unusual sight to see three cloaked women walking through the deserted streets of Jerusalem at such an early hour. It was too late for the women of the night, but too early for the emergence of the commercial world and all its traffic. An old man lay sleeping in a dirty doorway and a woman shrouded with a ragged cloak scurried away as they approached. A half starved fox rummaged in a pile of rubbish by a low stone wall. In the distance a cock screeched it's welcome to the coming morn. Mary Magdalene clutched the spices with which she intended to anoint the body of her friend and Lord. Mary the mother of Jesus walked arm in arm with her sister, Salome. She approached the prospect of viewing the shrouded body of her son with considerable trepidation although she also mysteriously felt a parallel emotion which could only be described as excitement. She occasionally gave way to a nervous little laugh as they walked which understandably attracted a quizzical look from her sister.

They passed through the Fish Gate and were heading north towards the place called Golgotha when a strange, loud, but distant thunder filled the air. It was enough to arrest the progress of the women. They stood motionless as an increasing violence of sound and motion caused the rocks to creak and groan beneath their feet. A sudden wind became the precursor to a fearful agitation of the ground which seemed to gently rise and fall with a vibration which grew in velocity until it reached a terrifying crescendo before diminishing to a stillness which was as silent as the grave. The earthquake lasted for no more than a minute and when it was over only the sound of dogs barking inside the city walls and the pounding of the hearts of the women remained as a reminder of the passing shaking of the earth. Arm in arm the loyal followers of Jesus tentatively continued their pilgrimage to the place of death.

It was impossible not to mentally relive the painful journey they had endured three days before. They were just a lonely trio now but Mary could still hear the cries of the crowd as her son, bruised and bleeding, was led as a lamb to the slaughter. In the eerie silence of the dawn, now more obvious in the wake of the violence of the quake, their sandals produced a strange scourging sound as they climbed the rocky terrain. Mary found herself searching the ground for blood marks left by her son. It occurred to her that they had nobody to roll away the stone from the mouth of the tomb. Perhaps they were a little unprepared for their visit or maybe if they all pushed together they might be able to move it. There was of course the added problem of the Roman guard and the official seal, and she knew that it was unlikely that they would receive any mercy or consideration from that quarter.

They were able to reach their destination without climbing Golgotha. The garden nestled at the foot of the rock upon which Jesus died, literally a stone's throw from the place of execution. The sun was beginning to expose its curve above the hills of Judea as the women nervously entered the silent, now sacred place. It was deserted. There was no sign of soldiers but more amazingly the heavy stone was already rolled back from the mouth of the tomb. Mary Magdalene, who was already in a state of emotional turmoil and much disturbed by the earthquake, cried out in horror at the sight, assuming that the body of her Lord had been stolen away. The box containing the anointing oils slipped from her grasp, scattering the contents across the rocky ground, and she turned to run.

"I'll go and fetch the men," she called over her shoulder and before anyone could protest she was out of the gate and running down the slope back towards Jerusalem.

Emotion pounded through Mary's veins. Adrenalin surged and energised her being. Dread and excitement in alternate waves swept through her chest as she ran to the mouth of the cave. She slowed down, calmed herself, and stepped inside, Salome close behind her. She silently absorbed its emptiness. The corpse of her son was gone. In the place where they had laid it three days earlier there sat two young men, clothed in long white garments, with altruistic, albeit imposing countenance. Fear gripped the timorous hearts of both women. This was not what they expected. The tomb was open, the body gone and two strange men were sitting as silent sentinels in the darkened cave. Their hearts shuddered and fainted with fear. What strange, supernatural happenings were these? And who were these strangers sitting in a tomb at such an early hour? One of the men sought to reassure them. His voice was gentle.

"Be not affrighted: ye seek Jesus of Nazareth, which was crucified: He is risen; He is not here: behold the place where they laid Him. But go your way, tell His disciples and Peter that He goeth before you into Galilee: there shall ye see Him."

It was one of those moments when it seems as though a thousand emotions pool their efforts to eliminate reason. Mary stood motionless for what seemed like an eternity, excitement and belief struggling for supremacy over fear and confusion. Then she found herself running. She could hear the sound of Salome running behind her. They fled with fear from the garden, out onto the dirt road and back towards the city, stopping only to catch their breath when they were a safe distance from the perplexing scene. The morning light was now established and served to wash away the ghostly uncertainties of the darkness.

They were walking briskly back towards John's house when they saw two men running towards them. The streets were now occupied with people making their way to their places of employment. Roman soldiers were mobilising for the boring daily patrols. The sun was threatening another hot day and the noise of chariot wheels gave expression to the dust which they kicked into the morning air. Peter and John were gasping from the effort of their run, but paused to listen as the women told them what they had seen and about the words of the angels. They had already met up with Mary Magdalene and were on their way to the tomb to see for themselves. They ran off into the distance and the two sisters, now free of fear, allowed the amazing words which they heard at the Garden Tomb to create the optimism and excitement for which they were intended. They made their way back to the house where the others were waiting and told them everything they knew. Mary Magdalene had already left to return to the tomb.

It was several hours before Peter and John returned. John was the first to arrive and told Mary that he believed that her son had been raised from the dead.

"It's the way the grave clothes were," he said. "Nobody has unwrapped the corpse because the shroud is still intact. His body must have somehow come through it because it has definitely not been unwound. And the soudarion was also still in place, not unravelled as it would be if someone had removed it. It is a miracle. He has risen, just as He said He would."

A wave of elation swept through a mother's heart. The Christ, her son, was raised from the dead. The emaciated broken form of Jesus was now raised by an astounding miracle from the dead. The future suddenly burst with optimism. The dragon was at last defeated. In that amazing moment she felt like the reason for her birth had been accomplished, her life work completed. Scriptures concerning the Messiah which once perplexed and confused her suddenly made sense. In fact the whole canon of Holy Writ became clear in a moment of revelation. It was all about her son. It was all about this world-changing moment. He, the true Passover Lamb was raised from the dead to act as High Priest and present His own blood as the atonement for the sins of the people. Magnificent! What a plan! The years of suffering, the hours of deepest agony, were now worthwhile. She spoke out loud the words her beloved Jesus had used just three days before on the cross, but she spoke them with new understanding. "It is finished! It is finished!" She gazed into the face of her new adopted son, John, and with a smile as bright as the sun she said again, "It is finished!"

Peter burst in upon the rejoicing pair with his face ruddy and sweaty from his run through the city streets and radiant with joy and excitement.

"I have seen Him," he shouted. "I have seen the Lord!" He put his strong hands on the shoulders of Mary and looked earnestly into her eyes. "I saw Him. I was on my way out of the garden after John left and He was standing before me. He just looked at me and gave a sad little smile. He didn't speak, but I know it was Him. He turned and walked slowly back into the garden. He's alive Mary. Jesus is alive."

"I think you're all mad."
The voice came from behind them and the three of them simultaneously turned to find Thomas and the rest of the group standing with disapproving expressions and openly exuding pessimism and unbelief. Thomas was their spokesman.

"You are all seeing what you want to see. You saw Him die, didn't you? You have told me of His torn body, the bones protruding through His flesh, and how the soldier plunged the spear into His heart. Nobody can come back from that. It is impossible. The fact is that they have removed His body so that we cannot. They will wait until you have all proclaimed a resurrection and then produce His body to make us all look like fools. It is madness to build your hopes up like this. It is a fantasy. Let it go. Let Him go. It's over."

The others stood sombre-faced, slowly nodding their heads to the reasoning's of logic. They all knew that Thomas was talking good sense. Mary and Peter and John were too emotionally involved. Nobody doubted that they really believed that Jesus was raised from the dead, but it was a delusion. For their own sakes they needed to accept the truth.

"He is alive, Thomas. I also have seen him."
Mary Magdalene had walked in as Thomas was speaking and was standing with her back to the door which she had closed behind her. Her voice was soft and controlled.

"At first I thought he was the gardener, but then He spoke my name. I wanted to hold Him, but He told me I could not because first He had to ascend to his Father. I don't understand what He meant, but I absolutely know that it was Him. He is alive!"
Thomas curled his lip with contemptuous disdain.
"If you are so sure that it was Him then why did you think He was the gardener?" He did not wait for an answer. "You practically admit that it did not look like Him. You say that you only knew when He spoke to you. It's all nonsense and I'll hear no more of it. You are all quite crazy and I'm leaving. Believe what you want to believe."
He pushed passed his friends and slammed the door behind him.

The atmosphere absorbed the conflict that silently raged between belief and unbelief. Inevitably two separate groups evolved, both conversing in undertones, one indulging in the restrained chatter of excitement, the other in murmurings of unbelief. Darkness was spreading its curtain across the evening sky before they were eventually pulled together by the arrival of two relatively unknown disciples of Jesus, Cleopas and his friend, who claimed that they also had seen Jesus. They were on their way to Emmaus when a stranger drew alongside them and chatted to them as they walked. They did not recognise Him at first, but when they reached the town they invited Him in for something to eat and He broke the bread exactly as He had done in the upper room when they ate the last supper with Jesus before he died. The group of believers found in this account another confirmation for their faith but unfortunately, for those who chose to be sceptical, it was more fuel for their fires of doubt.

The ensuing debate was cut short by a happening which silenced every tongue and blew away every last scrap of unbelief. It was one of those occasions when human beings sense the presence of another person in a room without seeing them. They all felt it at the same moment and they all turned together, and there, standing in the corner of the room, serene with august dignity, eminently regal and very much alive, was their friend and master, Jesus of Nazareth. Some of them still held back, trembling with fear as the last remnants of unbelief told them that they were seeing an apparition, some ghostly figment of their imagination. He smiled and said, "Peace be unto you." He showed them the nail marks in his hands and feet and pulled back his tunic to show them the scar in his side where the spear had torn Him open. Peter stood with those who had doubted, not because he doubted, but because he was ashamed of his cowardice and the unforgiveable betrayal of his friend. Mary slowly approached her son with tears of joy streaming down her face. She touched first His shoulders with the gentlest brushing of her palms and then his scarred face with her fingertips and then she was holding Him in her arms and weeping into His chest.

"Welcome home my son, my Lord," she whispered.

He did not reply, but she knew what the answer was. He had not come home. This was no longer His home. At that moment she knew that her time with Him would be very brief. His work here was done and soon He would be going to His true home, back to His Father. And as much as she wanted to keep Him she knew that now she really must finally let Him go.

CHAPTER TWENTY SEVEN

She saw Him several times over the next few weeks but everything was so palpably different. He was like a visitor, not just to her, but to them all. Nobody knew where He lived, where He stayed the night, or when He was just suddenly going to appear. He was obviously physical because they could touch Him, see his scars, and He ate food with them, but there was also something supernatural about Him. He was no longer subject to natural laws. Sometimes Mary even wondered if He was actually somehow already living back with His Father and commuting to Jerusalem or Galilee or wherever it was that He was next seen. One thing was obvious to her and it was not something she found easy to adjust to, but it seemed like she was no longer His mother. She knew that she was, and that she always would be, but it no longer felt like it. As the weeks passed she realised that she had more of a mother-son relationship with her nephew, John, than she did with Jesus. Perhaps that was why Jesus gave them to each other at the cross.

She was present when Jesus appeared to the disciples again a week after resurrection Sunday, the day that Thomas, who for a whole week had stubbornly refused to believe that they had actually seen the real Jesus, finally threw himself at the feet of his Lord. Peter told Mary the story of how Jesus appeared to them on the sea shore after five of them had spent a fruitless night of fishing on the lake and how He had made them breakfast and finally challenged and forgiven Peter for his failure. "Feed my sheep,"

He had said to him. She was there with her son, James, and the disciples on the mountain slopes in Galilee when Jesus appeared and talked with over five hundred of His followers at the same time.

She was there for the most amazing post-resurrection appearance of Jesus when He finally departed the world He came to save, when for the last time on this earth she looked upon her first-born son and said her last goodbye. A group of them had set out from Jerusalem on the road to Bethany and at a specific spot on the Mount of Olives Jesus called a halt and turned to face the Jerusalem He loved. It was from this mount that He once wept over the city he had come to save because of its unbelief. It was here that He knelt and prayed with such agony in the Garden of Gethsemane on the night of His betrayal, and He was very much aware that this was the very place to which He is destined to return on that wonderful future day when He will come as King and His feet will again touch the Mount of Olives. He could have also told them that here on this sacred ground He would one day set up His throne and bring peace and security to a turbulent world.

She watched as He ascended, hoping for that last special smile reserved for her and her alone, hoping that their eyes would meet across the widening divide, that she could hold them with her own until the clouds embraced Him and the curtain closed, but His eyes were on the city which lay behind them and they seemed to betray a unique blend of love and sadness and unspeakable triumph. Then she could almost hear the words prophesied by the psalmist ringing from the courts of the Eternal World,

"Lift up your heads O ye gates, and be ye lifted up, ye everlasting doors; and the King of Glory shall come in. Who is this King of Glory? The Lord strong and mighty, the Lord mighty in battle. Lift up your heads, O ye gates; even lift them up ye everlasting doors; and the King of Glory shall come in. Who is this King of Glory? The Lord of hosts, He is the King of Glory."

She could imagine the sound of trumpets, a wonderful fanfare of triumphant music to welcome Him home. His final words to them concerned the legacy He had left, an opportunity for salvation for all mankind.

"Wait in Jerusalem," He had said, "until the power comes. Then take the Gospel to the world. Preach it everywhere."

The spiritual woman that she was felt fulfilled and exhilarated with the writing of this final chapter of God's visit to His creation in the form of man, but as a mother she experienced such deep sadness. Memories flooded her mind as the insignificant looking group of friends turned back and began their descent into Jerusalem, memories of His lowly birth, the slaughter of the innocents, the flight to Egypt, the boy learning to cut wood with His father in the carpentry, the day she found her boy conversing with the doctors in the Temple, the picture of Him standing with such dignity at the funeral of her beloved Joseph. There were too many memories for her to cope with and her emotions broke through her resistance and she felt the hand of her given son, John, around her shoulder as the tears coursed down her cheeks and her bosom heaved with sobs.

They all waited in Jerusalem according to the Lord's instructions, about one hundred and twenty of them. They stayed in the upper room where they had met for the last supper. They prayed and sang psalms and fellowshipped together for a full ten days before the power came. It came in the form of the promised Comforter, the Holy Spirit, whom Jesus had promised to send as His replacement on the earth. Mary had, of course, met Him before, this third person of the Godhead, on that awesome night when He visited and overshadowed her and planted in her womb the seed of the Messiah. Now, on the day of Pentecost, He came to them all with such power that it shook the very building they were in. With the sound of a rushing mighty wind He came and filled them and the room with His overwhelming presence. It was a special moment in the Divine purpose for the world. It was the birth of the empowered church, the beginning of evangelism, and the impact of it was to be felt around the world.

Mary rejoiced above all others at the growth of the Kingdom of Jesus Christ. Three thousand followers of Jesus were added on that first day of visitation, and it went on every day after it. The church in Jerusalem grew with unbelievable rapidity. Signs and wonders and astonishing miracles were happening everywhere, in the Temple, in the home, and in the streets. It was like a revolution. The very thing that the Jewish leaders had conspired to prevent by seeking the crucifixion of Jesus was happening around them and now they had no idea what to do to stop it. Annas the high priest ordered the arrest of Peter and John and called them to answer before himself and his kindred. They threatened them that they must cease to preach and teach in the name of Jesus, but they had no choice but to release them for fear of the people. Within a short time the growth of the church was so enormous and the miracles so popular with the people that the religious leaders were afraid they were losing control. People were now bringing their sick families and friends into the streets and faith was rising so high that they believed that if just the shadow of Peter fell across them they would be healed. Peter and John were arrested for a second time and on this occasion they were in danger of losing their lives. Only through the intervention of a man called Gamaliel did they escape death, but they were subjected to a fearful scourging which left them torn and bleeding and scarred for life.

This was only the beginning of a prolonged persecution against the Church which lasted for years. A wonderful follower of Jesus by the name of Stephen, who had great faith and worked many wonders and miracles amongst the people was arrested, falsely accused, and stoned to death. A Pharisee by the name of Saul of Tarsus, a powerful and influential man, presided over Stephen's execution and proceeded to round up Christians and have them imprisoned or put to death. The persecution of the followers of Jesus was growing as fast as the Church and Peter and John began to fear for the life of Mary. If these enemies of Jesus could succeed in apprehending and killing His mother it would be a major triumph and a huge blow against the spread of the Gospel. There was some good news in the midst of the horror of those days when Mary heard of the astonishing conversion of their arch enemy Saul of Tarsus who was evidently confronted with a vision of Christ whilst on his way to Damascus to apprehend

Christians. Many in the church thought that the so-called conversion was an elaborate plot designed to lure Christians into a trap and refused to believe that Saul was now a follower of Jesus, but Mary rejoiced that one who had hated Christ so passionately was now a committed preacher of the Gospel. Time would indeed produce the evidence to validate the conversion of one of the most influential Christians in the whole of history.

Following the regeneration of Saul, who became universally known as Paul, the Church did experience a time of relative relief from the worst of the persecution, but when Emperor Tiberius died in March AD37 his successor Caligula immediately appointed Herod Agrippa to the kingship of the province of Syria, the first Jew to be called king since his grandfather Herod the Great. As a close friend of Caligula he stayed for some time in Rome and did not actually arrive in his kingdom until July of AD38. When Caligula was murdered in Rome on 24th January AD41 the Jewish king played an important role during the accession of Claudius and as a reward for his loyalty the territories of Judea and Samaria were added to his kingdom and Jerusalem once again became the capital of a united Palestine. Agrippa was a man jealous of his own power and anxious to please the Jews and in the pursuit of this he engaged in active opposition against the church.

It was in the Spring of AD44 and Salome was sitting chatting with her sister, Mary, and her son, John, when she heard the news that her eldest son, James, had been arrested. Although it was a long time ago she had never forgotten the haunting vision which she had seen in the swirling mountain mist whilst sailing Lake Galilee with her husband Zebedee and her three year old son. The sickening reality of the ethereal decapitation she witnessed that day now surged into her mind like a tidal wave. Deep down she had known on that terrifying morning on the lake that she was experiencing a visual premonition of a future tragedy, but across the years she controlled her fear and with a little success convinced herself that it was a figment of her imagination. As the frightened young messenger delivered his news she knew now that the past had caught up with the present. A lump rose in her throat and fear clawed at her chest.

"This is it, Mary," she whispered. "It's over. I will never see my son again."

She wept silently for several minutes before calmly raising her head. She spoke firmly to Mary, like an older sister does when she wants to make it clear that she will not take no for an answer.

"You must leave, dear sister. It is only a matter of time before they come for you."

She turned to John whose face was ashen white with concern for the brother he loved. She tenderly took his hand in hers.

"Take her away, John. Save her life."

She saw the agony in the eyes of her son. She was challenging him to leave his mother and only brother to face their darkest hour alone in order to rescue her sister. She knew it was the most difficult thing he had ever been asked to do. His face was disfigured with a convolution of emotional anguish.

"John, remember the words of the Master. He gave His mother to you for your protection as He was giving his life so willingly for us. You must do this for Him. You must do it for us all. I will lose two sons today and it will break my heart, but I love my Lord enough to do it. I know you love Him too."

The following morning James the son of Zebedee was led to the place of execution shackled to his guard, a tall middle-aged man by the name of Julius. James was the very essence of courage, bright and confident in the face of death. He radiated a joy and peace which was reminiscent of the man whom Julius had personally executed by decapitation with the sword thirteen years before in the cave prison of Machaeus. He never forgot the way that John the Baptist prayed for his executioner before he knelt submissively before his sword, or the powerful 'Hallelujah' which launched him into eternity. Julius spoke quietly to James as they walked together towards the locale of death.
"A man called John the son of Zacharias once told me about the love of Jesus of Nazareth. I was his guard and executioner. He said that Jesus was the Messiah. He was so calm in the face of death. Like you, sir. You carry the same aura of peace. I met His mother you know, the mother of Jesus I mean. She came to visit him at Machaeus on the night he died."

They arrived at the site where James must die and the soldier was ordered to remove the shackles and stand clear. He stood for a moment in silent contemplation before slowly kneeling at the feet of his prisoner.

"Sir," he said in a voice that could be heard by all present, "I believe that Jesus of Nazareth is the Messiah and that He died for my sins. I believe that God raised Him from the dead and I pledge myself to follow Him for as long as I live."

A stunned silence dominated the scene of judgement, eventually broken by the rough voice of the officer in command.
"You will not follow Him for long you bloody fool," he roared. Uproarious laughter greeted his contemptuous response. The officer waved his hand in cruel finality.
"Kill them both."
They knelt, still shackled together, now as brothers, and James pronounced this benediction upon his friend.
"Peace my son, peace be to thee and the pardon of thy faults."
The sword flashed as Salome had foreseen and sent her son and his companion into the presence of their Lord.

Two days later Simon Peter was arrested and sentenced to death. The danger to Mary was now critical and John, now utterly committed to do what he had to do to save her, urged her to depart. With a breaking heart he kissed his grieving mother a fond farewell and with tears dampening his ample beard watched the two dearest women in his life hold each other in their last embrace. Somehow they both knew that they would never meet again.

That night, the same night that Peter was being miraculously released from his prison, John and Mary, heavily cloaked for fear of being recognised and arrested, slipped out of

Jerusalem and took flight for Antioch and the safety of the anonymity it afforded them. Paul and Barnabas were leaders of a growing church in the city and John knew that they would look after them. He also knew that it would not be safe to stay there for a prolonged period. He had no idea where they would go from there but he was at peace in his spirit and content to trust God for guidance. They would all pray for direction and follow whatever the guiding hand of the Almighty indicated for their future service.

CHAPTER TWENTY EIGHT

The rattling grind of chariot wheels against the cobbles and the cry of street vendors plying their wares rose spasmodically above the general chatter of the populace on a hot afternoon in Ephesus. Slaves carrying heavy crates of fruit in preparation for the festival later in the day were making their way along the impressive avenue known as Harbour Street towards the north gate of the Grand Theatre. The breathtaking open-air auditorium, seating up to 24,000 people, was to be a significant landmark on the route of the festival procession. The market square, known as the Lower Agora, was teaming with activity. Stalls selling idol deities of differing size, shape and significance were everywhere. Flower girls were selling their produce fresh from the fields and figs, olives, and grapes, all grown in the rich fertile soil of the surrounding landscape, were to be had in abundance. A fresh cargo of slaves was being sold for sacks of salt, harvested in pans from the sea. A profitable slave was said to be "worth his salt", an expression still used in today's world to express the value of a good worker.

This was Ephesus, the celebrated cosmopolitan city of Ionia in Asia Minor, sprawling impressively across the mouth of the River Cayster, the source of water for this most beautiful part of the province. Although Pergamum was the formal capital of Asia, Ephesus was now the centre of the Roman government and the residence of the proconsul and his staff. The natural harbour established the city as the major port of Ionia and the population had risen to 250,000 souls. In the reign of Emperor Augustus Ephesus became the epitome of civilisation and Asia's largest metropolis. At the core of her life and fame stood the magnificent temple of the goddess Diana (Artemis). The breathtaking edifice stood like an ominous guard at the head of the harbour, its 130ft high structure, 350ft long and 180ft wide, supported on no less than 137 magnificently carved pillars. The temple is still remembered for its status as one of the seven wonders of the ancient world. Paussanias, renowned historian of the time, describing this architectural masterpiece, said, "I have seen the Hanging Gardens of Babylon, the statue of Olympian Zeus, The Colossus of Rhodes, The Pyramids of Egypt, the Light House of Alexandria and the Mausoleum of Halicarnassus. But, when I have seen the Temple of Artemis towering to the clouds, all the other wonders diminishingly lost their grandeur. The most beautiful work ever created by human kind."

Ephesus was the ancient city of the arts, where costume and theatre, music, mysticism and leisure were valued above most other things and where the learned, many of them Jews, frequented the city library which lay not far from the market square if accessed through the Monumental Gate of the Agora. It was a city of slave labour where human beings were treated no better than animals, no less than 20,000 of them working in the iron, zinc, silver, and lead mines in the surrounding hills, always subject to the foreman's whip, and attempting to escape at peril to their lives.

Today, the thirteenth day of August in the year 44AD was a special day, the date set aside for the annual Feria of the

Nemoralia (festival of torches). The streets were teeming with people who had come from near and far to attend the festival of Diana. The volume of traffic passing through the splendid wharfs and docks in the harbour was astonishing. The water was teeming with colourful flotillas of boats large and small, some obviously military, but most of them commercial, and more than the usual number of private boats carrying passengers on their way to pay homage to the famous goddess. Thousands of young women from across the province were amongst the crowds. They had made the pilgrimage in the hope of receiving a miracle from Diana, goddess of motherhood and fertility, hoping for fruit from their barren wombs. Others who were already pregnant were there in the hope of guaranteeing an easy and painless birth. Already people were pressing to kneel before the image of the idol which stood twelve feet tall on a platform before the entrance to the temple, its torso covered with row after row of multiple protruding breasts as a symbol of universal motherhood, and its lower half adorned with the carvings of animals to portray her reproductive powers for all living creatures. The temple was not regarded as her actual dwelling place, but rather as a shrine to her honour. She was believed to live in Nature as the mother of all living things. She was severally called the white moon goddess of light, goddess of the wild, the divine huntress, protector of animals, goddess of fertility, and more significantly, the virgin queen of heaven.

The festival began in the late afternoon. Two hundred and sixty virgin priestesses attractively adorned with wreathes of flowers around their necks and with flowers elaborately woven into their braided hair led the procession carrying thirty-one gold and silver statues, nine of them of Diana. They walked in step slowly from the temple to a place outside the city walls and then circled round to the Magnesian Gate which was the main entrance to Ephesus from the south. Here they were joined by a company of adolescent males called "Ephebes", young men of considerable social status chosen to enhance the proceedings. With solemn ceremony and accompanied by melancholy strains of haunting music the young people entered the city and the crowds began to chant, first in a haunting, hushed whisper, then with increasing volume, "Great is Diana of the Ephesians." The procession was slow, impeded by the steadily growing throng, but made its way to the Amphitheatre where over twenty thousand people waited for the arrival of the virgins. Here offerings of flowers and plants, wormwood, jasmine, lavender, mandrake, rosemary and hazel were laid upon the stage with cakes of honey, parsley, wheat and barley, together with offerings of milk and unmixed wine and other sacrificial cakes. Prayers were read pleading that the goddess would help the women in childbirth, protect the animals in their habitat, and give fruit to the vine. A hymn in praise of Diana of the Glades, mistress of the rolling hills and babbling brooks, was sung as the sun dipped gracefully into the sea. Thousands of lamps now flickered in the half light, each candle burning more brightly with the advance of darkness as the procession made its way back to the Temple of Diana. The worship now became a sordid brand of religious hysteria as the crowd bayed for the blood of animal sacrifice.

Open flame torches now burned to light the scene as a struggling steer was dragged to the altar and its throat sliced open to the excited cries of the people. The smell of hot blood seemed to intoxicate the worshippers and arouse them to frightening levels of unrestrained lust. Naked women danced and swayed to the music of the pipes with reckless abandonment as the temple prostitutes moved amongst the people to provide opportunity for prurient men to worship Diana with the public release of lewd and carnal passion. Scenes of depraved lasciviousness beckoned demonic powers to incite unspeakable acts of debauchery. The night of blood and violence and sex and an exhibition of morals beneath those of animals and the dark activities of sorcerers plying their trade in public exorcisms and muttered incantations made the morning blush with shame as the crowds eventually dispersed and Ephesus stood silent and sleepy before the coming day.

A merchant ship rode slowly into port, its sales flapping loosely in the breeze. It was three weeks since her departure from Sidon in Phoenicia. The Corbita had sailed around the northern coast of Cyprus to the city of Myra in Lycia, a journey of some nine days. Following a two-night stopover she sailed on to the Greek Island of Rhodes and finally to Ephesus. There was no indication of the city's previous night's revelry as the crew fastened the moorings and informed the only two passengers on board that it was time to disembark. The couple who stepped nervously over the crude landing stage onto dry land looked tired and somewhat bewildered. This was for them a new world, a new culture, unlike anything they had experienced before. They had nowhere to go and little money to buy food, let alone lodgings. They stood together arm in arm and gazed at the towering Temple of Diana which imposed itself on the eyes of every visitor who accessed Ephesus from the sea. To these two it stood as a challenge to their faith. Who was the more powerful, this idol deity who incited men and women to evil beyond comprehension, or the little known Jesus of Nazareth with his message of purity and self discipline? Who would conquer in this magnificent Roman port, the world celebrated goddess of motherhood who was misguidedly called the virgin queen of heaven, or the one who in the purity of her youth had become the virgin mother of the Christ? Mary, now a woman of sixty years and as poor in this world's goods as she was when the angel visited her back in Nazareth forty-five years before, gazed at the spectacular and extravagant wealth of Diana and sensed in the aura around her temple the dark spirit of the dragon. Her figure was still trim and healthy, but the lines of premature aging on her weary face were testimony to the path of suffering she had walked and her once black hair was now peppered with silver grey. She straightened her back and lifted her head with dignified defiance and a smile of acceptance edged her lips. She would accept the challenge, for had they not both felt that this was the place to come? She looked up into John's face and smiled. He knew before she spoke that she had no intention of allowing this place, or its goddess, to overcome her will.

"Well, John," she said. "This is our home and the place of our appointment and here we will build the Church of Jesus Christ. The day will come when that proud temple of idolatry and uncleanness will lie in ruins, but the name of Jesus will be honoured for all time throughout the world."

CHAPTER TWENTY NINE

They found lodgings in a small stone terraced house in the city centre not far from the agora. John had sufficient funds to pay in advance for the first month's rent and the day after their arrival he was traversing the docks looking for work on one of the local fishing boats. He had no problem finding employment once the owners became aware of his upbringing and expertise in the industry and he was soon bringing home more than enough finance to adequately care for Mary's needs. It was not easy to adjust to the culture of a society steeped in idolatry and turpitude, but they both knew that if the Gospel was to be taken to the world its preachers had to live in that world. Jesus had not told them to stay at home, but to "Go into all the world" and that meant that they needed to adjust to living with different attitudes and ways of life. They found a small makeshift Synagogue where a number of Jews met on the Sabbath and began to attend. It was an opportunity to share with their fellow countrymen matters concerning the Messiah and the things that had happened in Jerusalem, but the Jews were not easily persuaded and certainly not hasty to believe.

John enjoyed his work. It was so exhilarating to once more feel the moving ship beneath his feet, the fresh wind blowing the spray into his face, and to hear and feel the gentle creaking of the timbers as he occupied himself in the business he knew so well. It was like old times. All he needed was Peter and Andrew to share the experience and of course his brother, James. His eyes filled with tears as he thought of his dear brother and the price he had paid for his loyalty to his Lord. He also felt more than a little guilty for feeling so content with his lot. He was always aware that he was not called to fish the Aegean Sea, but the great sea of humanity, to rescue the souls of men. He just hoped that God understood that at the moment he had no choice but to work the boats if he was to be obedient to the plea that Jesus had made to him from His cross to care for Mary. As the months passed he was disquietened about Mary living in lodgings in the middle of the metropolis and began to entertain ambitions to build her a home of her own on the outskirts of the city. He was the youngest of all the apostles, still only thirty-two years of age and as strong as an ox. He would find it a joy to carry stone and timber and build a home worthy of the woman who produced the Christ.

A year later he climbed the hill Bulbul on the outskirts of Ephesus and stood in a clearing amidst the olive and pine trees and looked out over the sea far below. He had walked quite a distance from the town and it was as though civilisation did not exist. It was the most peaceful and beautiful place he had ever seen and he instinctively knew that this was the place where he would build a dwelling place for the mother of his Lord. He spent the next eighteen months working on the boats during the night and carrying and building during the day, spending only a few hours in his bed. At times of great weariness and exhaustion he reminded himself of the agony endured by his Lord as he looked down from the cross and said "Son, behold thy mother" and with renewed enthusiasm he gave himself to the task. By the summer of AD47 the house was finished and simply furnished in preparation for a viewing by his much loved aunt.

She wept as she stepped inside, not just in gratitude for John's practical expression of love, but because of the presence of the Holy Spirit of peace which filled her new home.
"A long way from my childhood home in Nazareth," she smiled. "So different from the carpentry I loved so well. Yet how beautiful is this place. How sweet the presence of my Lord. Thank you John. Thank you so much for all your labour of love. Here we will have our home and from here you will do the will of God wherever He may send you. You must not feel obligated to always be here. There is a task to be done in the cause of Jesus and we must both work for its accomplishment."

John left Mary and returned to Israel in 49AD to the first Council of Jerusalem. It was great to see the apostles and elders, Paul and Barnabas, and James the brother of Jesus who was now the leader of the Jerusalem church, and of course his old friend, Peter, who had recently returned from Rome. James wanted to know how his mother was and he was thrilled to hear of the mountain home his friend had built for her.
"I must come and see her", he said. Then, somewhat apologetically, he added "God willing." Salome came to visit her son and held him in her arms for an eternity, weeping gently onto his strong shoulder. She was an old lady now, looking even older than her seventy-two years. John sensed a deep sadness in his aged mother, but knew that it was a condition which she would never acknowledge. She seemed

lonely and he suspected that she had never truly recovered from the violent death of his brother, James.

"How good you look, John. Why, you are more handsome than ever. Is my sister well? Tell her I think of her and pray for her every day."
"I will tell her, mother, and yes, she is very well, though like you she has rather more grey hairs than she would like. Her spirit is alive in communion with God and that keeps her young in heart."
He handed her the letter which Mary had written to her sister some weeks before and Salome sat reading the familiar handwriting, occasionally pausing to wipe a tear from her eye.

John, loaded with letters for Mary from many old friends, kissed his mother and set out for the return journey to Ephesus just a week after his fellow apostles returned from the Council to their respective areas of service. Paul was planning to embark upon his second missionary journey with his colleague Silas and was anxious to get back to Antioch to finalise their plans. John found Ephesus alive with the news from Rome that the emperor Claudius had issued an edict commanding all Jews to leave the city without delay. This was sensational as it was appalling for it displaced many thousands of people and was guaranteed to produce untold suffering. John could not help thinking that the main target for the attack was the speedily growing and more active group of Christian Jews in Rome. When Paul arrived in Corinth a year later he found two of these exiled Jews actively preaching Christ in the city. Their names were Priscilla and Aquila and, like Paul, they were skilled tentmakers. They immediately allied with the apostle and they worked together for a full eighteen months, preaching the Gospel and building the church. It was during this period that Paul wrote two inspirational letters to the church at Thessalonica. In the summer of 52AD Priscilla and Aquila accompanied Paul to Ephesus. After a brief visit and some sweet fellowship with John and Mary, Paul left for Caesarea, leaving Aquila and his wife to help with the establishing of the church in Ephesus, but not before he had made a powerful impact upon the worshippers in the synagogue who tried to persuade him to stay longer. Mary was greatly encouraged by Paul and very grateful for the help of the strong and established couple whom he brought to work in the city.

Days were long and somewhat lonely in the mountain and John was a little too protective of Mary and was uneasy whenever she ventured into the city. He took her every Sabbath to the synagogue where a number of people had acknowledged Jesus as their Messiah. Priscilla and Aquila were forthright and passionate in their adherence to the Gospel and bold in its proclamation. John, although strong and supportive in the infant church, considered his main duty to care for Mary although he did take a few weeks to visit Rome where he put himself in considerable danger at a time when Christians were regarded as a subversive nuisance. Mary was a woman of prayer and spent most of her days in communion with her Lord. She cultivated a perceptive spirit and an understanding of the divine mind which were invaluable to the developing church. She was the first to sense danger and John learned to listen carefully when she voiced her concerns. When she heard in the spring of 54AD of the murder of Claudius, news which was received with some relief by thousands of her Jewish countrymen, and that the sixteen year old Lucius Domitius Ahenobarbus, great grandson of Caesar Augustus and better known as Nero, had acceded to the throne, she turned pale with horror.

"But Mary," John reasoned, "He cannot possibly be worse than Claudius. Remember what he did to the Jews in Rome."

"Believe me John; if how I feel is right, this man is of far greater danger to those who love Jesus than Claudius ever was and more wicked than any before him."

She was of course completely correct. The cruel and vile man Nero was destined to rank as one of the most evil men who ever lived and went to his suicide grave with the blood of thousands of Christians to his account.

Later that year brought another enthusiastic preacher to Ephesus. A Jew by the name of Apollos, born in Alexandria in north central Egypt, a man of superb knowledge of the scriptures and unequalled in eloquence and the power of oratory, arrived at the Synagogue and fervently preached Christ to the people. Aquila and Priscilla noticed that his preaching seemed to indicate that his understanding of baptism was not mature, that to him baptism represented only repentance from sin as preached by John the Baptist rather than the deeper meaning of Christian baptism which symbolised the end of the old life and the receiving of the new nature through the second birth as preached by Jesus to a ruler of the Jews by the name of Nicodemus. They took him aside and explained to him the difference and with the humility of one truly following Christ he thanked them for their help. He left quite an impact on the emerging church in Ephesus before leaving for Corinth. Two weeks after his departure Paul arrived by land having departed from Antioch and passed through Iconium on his third missionary journey.

The timing was perfect. Not only was he able to now baptise the converts to Christ with more profound meaning, baptising them into the wonder of the Godhead, but was also able to introduce them to baptism in the Holy Spirit. Both John and Mary were ecstatic. Paul seemed in no hurry to move on and the church entered a period of sustained growth. For three months he preached Christ in the Synagogue until a number of the hardened Jewish traditionalists who did not believe made things impossible and he moved out, taking the new Christians with him. He and John and Mary then ministered to the people, holding services in the house of a man named Tyrannus. The power of God was now displayed in Diana's domain and special miracles were done by Paul in the name of Jesus. Faith grew so strong that people were actually sending handkerchiefs and aprons to the house for Paul to pray over and later when they were laid upon the sick people miracles of healing took place. It was a sensation and news spread throughout the city as the number of disciples increased. People who were involved in witchcraft and the curious arts of Diana were turning to Christ and brought their idols and books and publicly burned them.

Mary was both thrilled and nervous. She knew that the spread of Christianity in Ephesus and beyond was guaranteed to stir up opposition from the thousands who made huge amounts of money from the worship of Diana. Paul had been with them for almost two and a half years and was already talking of a return to Jerusalem and she was not sure how John was going to cope with the aftermath of Paul's ministry and the possible backlash. She made it a matter of much prayer and intercession.

In the early spring of 57AD Mary's worst fears were realised. The trouble originated from a silversmith named Demetrius who managed a business selling silver shrines for Diana to the Ephesians. He and the craftsmen he employed were making a fortune from their trade, a trade which was now being seriously threatened by the rapid increase of this new religion which taught that idol worship was wrong. They held a public meeting and accused the Christians of despising the sacred temple of Diana and of seeking its destruction. They proceeded to hold a public demonstration in the streets to the chant of "Great is Diana of the Ephesians" and the crowd grew to thousands strong, many of whom had no idea what the demonstration was about. It was utter confusion and chaos as the multitude swept into the amphitheatre, the mob having apprehended two of Paul's companions, Gaius and Aristarchus, two men from Macedonia. Paul wanted to go into the theatre after them, but his friends restrained him, fearing for his life. The noise was deafening as the people roared "Great is Diana of the Ephesians."

Mary could hear the sound of hatred in her home on the hill. It was as though the dragon was revitalised, as though the breath of demonic antagonism was setting the city on fire and would consume the church. How she prayed that day. She called upon the power of the Holy Spirit to subdue the mob and protect the lives of Paul and his friends. She had no idea where John was. All she could do was commit him into the care of the Father. She prayed until the cacophony slowly died and tranquillity presided over the city, then she prayed again for the safe return of her friends. She discovered on their return that the town clerk had entered the arena and called for the attention of the people. He skilfully praised the indomitable standing which Diana held in the affection of the people and assured them that her position was unassailable. He recommended to Demetrius and his friends that if they had a dispute they should take it up through the proper channels of the law and made it clear that he firmly opposed the mob mentality which he considered utterly unacceptable. The uproar was eventually subdued and the people dismissed to their homes. That night Paul called the church together and embraced the people, bidding them a fond farewell. As the dawn broke he departed for Macedonia.

CHAPTER THIRTY

As an elderly woman of seventy-four years Mary was reasonably active. Despite some aches and pains in her joints she was still able to visit the city and enjoy the fellowship of the growing church. It was a source of great joy to watch the growth of light in such a spiritually dark place. The church became a powerful influence in Ephesian society and adherents to the faith were added by the day. She was never a prominent figure, but with a wonderful ability to offer wise and gentle counsel to both ministry and people, and possessing an abundance of insight and discernment, she matured into an indispensable asset to the Christian community.

She spent the bulk of her time alone in her little home, but she was never lonely. Her communion with her Lord was the most important aspect of her life and the powerhouse of her effectiveness. The beauty of her environment and the gentle music of the spring of water which bubbled within a few strides of her door was nature's contribution to her peace. Not that she always enjoyed a state of tranquillity because she was always conscious of the spiritual battle which raged for the souls of men. She discovered that the unseen realm was very real and that if she was to positively influence the cause of her Son she must engage in supernatural battles which brought pressures and oppressions which could only be overcome by persistent prayer. If the power of witchcraft and soothsaying and the incantations of the priestesses of Diana were to be vanquished it was at a price. She was prepared to pay it, in prayer, and alone.

She never forgot the instruction of Jesus to embrace the whole world as her mission field. Although confined to one location her prayers were universal and she constantly pursued news of the various missions engaged by the apostles in different parts of the world. She prayed for Paul who was now in Corinth and then headed for Jerusalem. She sensed in her spirit that Paul was in danger of arrest and imprisonment. He had already suffered so much in the cause of the Gospel, five times having received thirty-nine stripes, three times beaten up with clubs, three times shipwrecked, once spending a whole day and night in the sea. She had seen the broken state of his body and the horrendous scars which told the story of the lacerating whip. For hours she earnestly prayed for this courageous little man and those who travelled with him. She prayed for Peter who was working with Mark in what is now Iraq, and for Matthew who was labouring somewhere in Ethiopia. She heard that her stepson, Jude, was preaching in Edessa. How she would love to see him. He reminded her so much of her beloved Joseph. She prayed for Mary Magdalene and all her friends from long ago. So it went on, always caring, always praying, and always listening to the still small voice of the Holy Spirit.

In the summer of 59 AD she heard that Paul had been arrested in Jerusalem and was now in prison in Caesarea. At first she reacted to the news with horror, but quickly found a state of peace. It seemed to her that this could all be part of the greater plan which would result in yet more benefits for the Kingdom of God. She committed him into the hands of the One who makes no mistakes, praying that Paul's afflictions would serve to purify and strengthen his character for time and eternity. She was not always brave and sometimes she endured times of sorrow and fear for her loved ones. When she received news in the January of 60 AD that her beloved sister Salome had passed away at the age of eighty-three years she refused all consolation. She knew that she was old and ready for departure and that none of us can last forever on this earth, but the memories were too many. She fell into a state of regret that she had ever left Israel. She mourned the years that she had missed the joy and laughter of her sibling. She mused of their days together in Galilee, the support Salome had been at the time of the crucifixion of Jesus, and the day they climbed arm in arm the rough stone steps of Machaeus to visit the imprisoned John the Baptist. She wept quietly for hours until eventually she had the wisdom and self-discipline to shake herself free of melancholy and leave the past where it belongs and look beyond the shores of time to a better world. Then she perceived with the inner eye of the spirit her sister, radiant and young, dancing like an angel around the throne of God and of the Lamb, and she heard music such as was never heard by human ear. Her tears of deep sorrow became those of transcendent joy and her little home once more became the house of peace.

She often longed, as any mother would, to see her son, James, still Bishop of Jerusalem, and following the news of the decease of her sister the desire grew stronger. She prayed that he would visit her and as the months passed she found herself from time to time imagining him opening the door and surprising her. She even spoke to John about returning to Israel for a visit, but he insisted that even if she were strong enough to make the journey the danger to her life was as great as it had ever been. She protested with a measure of indignance.

"But I don't care about my life. My usefulness in this world is at an end anyway, but I would like to see my son."

The loyal servant of Jesus caringly took her hand between his own.

"Mary, you would never make it. The journey by ship would be too arduous for you. You are not young anymore and there are still things for you to do here. Be patient. Maybe James will be able to come and see you before very long."

Unfortunately it was not to be. In the June of 62 AD she received the shocking and shattering news that James was dead.

Following the death of the procurator Porcius Festus, before his successor Lucceius Albinus took office, Ananus, the high priest in Jerusalem, seized his opportunity to call a meeting of the Sanhedrin and subsequently condemned James, with several others, as a lawbreaker. According to the historian Josephus, Ananus 'made the accusation that they had transgressed the law, and he handed them over to be stoned.' He had succeeded in his vile plot to destroy the leader of the Jerusalem church.

Mary was fully aware of the dreadful death that her beloved son had suffered. The bloody and prolonged death by stoning was grotesque and barbaric. She tried to close her perceptive mind to the scene of murderous brutality endured by her offspring, but each time she turned away she saw another stone flying through the air, felt another pain, and saw another source of blood. It was too much for her to take. The memory of the horror of Golgotha and the agony endured by her firstborn now fought for a place in her mind alongside the heinous suffering of her son, James. Two sons had issued from her womb and she had lived to know that they both met the most violent and undeserved deaths. She wailed her agony into the valley below and wept until her body ached with immeasurable grief. She cried for her long lost Joseph, but with the death of James the last piece of her husband was finally gone from the earth. She felt so utterly alone. She wanted to die. All John could do was to hold her frail and broken life in his arms and whisper a prayer for help to the God of all comfort.

When the initial pangs of incurable loss were somewhat abated Mary found a vestige of comfort in the bravery her son had reportedly shown in the face of death. He evidently prayed a prayer similar to the one Jesus prayed from His cross, "Father forgive them for they know not what they do," whereupon one of his persecutors cried out "Cease! What do ye? This just man is praying for us!" His protest fell upon deaf ears and soon afterwards the brother of our Lord found peace in His eternal presence.

How desperately the mother of the Saviour wanted to go home! She yearned for an escape route from this world of sadness and bad news. Nero was evil beyond description and his cruelty knew no bounds. Having already arranged the murder of his mother Agrippina in 59 AD he now proceeded to kill his wife Octavia so that he could marry his mistress Poppaea Sabina. Paul was now Nero's prisoner in Rome, although the apostle was resolute in affliction and the church at Ephesus had recently received an inspiring letter from him delivered by a faithful brother named Tychicus. The epistle did somewhat lift the spirit of the aged Mary. She was encouraged by Paul's unquenchable desire to preach the Gospel, even as a prisoner. In his letter he asked for prayer for boldness and declared himself to be "an ambassador in bonds." His buoyant attitude was a wonderful example and one which she was determined to follow, but she was weary with sorrow and her discernment told her that all did not bode well for the future.

It was the day following Mary's eightieth birthday that news reached Ephesus that the city of Rome was burning. Many Romans thought that the egotistic Nero, desperate to have his name forever etched into the architecture of the capital and centre of the empire, arranged for the city to be fired that he might rebuild it in his name. When rumours that he was responsible for the disaster spread through the city he answered them with a counter accusation against the Christian population and there began the most dreadful persecution of the followers of Jesus. The insane monster Nero, murderer and sexual deviant, guilty of incest (with his mother) and homo and heterosexual rape, now turned his sadistic fury against the Christians. Many of them were wrapped in animal skins and thrown to the dogs or lions in the Circus Maximus to be ripped to pieces. Others were crucified, and yet others were dipped in wax before being impaled on long staves in the gardens of the emperor to be set alight to serve as human torches. Rarely has time produced a man so universally base, the very embodiment of evil, and the antithesis of Christian culture.

Mary buried her face in her soft wrinkled hands and wept for the innocent lives that were being sacrificed for their love of her Son. She wanted to ask why? She wanted to object, to say it wasn't fair, or to ask her Heavenly Father why He did not intervene and stop the carnage. Then she remembered how her own flight from Israel had brought the Gospel to Asia and how scattered Christians preached the Word in Antioch and across Europe. She suddenly saw how that through the willing suffering and sacrifice of the church the message of salvation was spreading its mantle across the earth. Could it be that the horrendous nightmare perpetuated by the wicked Nero would have the effect of fulfilling the mission of the very people being persecuted? And what rewards would await them in the eternal world of everlasting light?

She was right. The burning Christians of Rome were lighting a fire that would never be put out. Because of the attention Nero attracted to the Church by persecuting it, and the undoubted courage and resolve of the people who were killed, who died with such grace and love, praying for their murderers as they expired, the entire empire became open to the Gospel and multitudes came to know the Saviour in the years which followed. For Mary, however, it was a matter of trust. She must just believe the witness of her spirit and by faith embrace the vision that, as Paul had written some years before to the Christians in Rome, "All things work together for good to them that love God, to them who are the called according to His purpose."

She was just eighty-three years old when John came back from Ephesus one afternoon with a sombre look upon his face. She could see that he had been weeping.
"What's wrong, John?" she asked, reaching out her hand for him to come to her. She found it difficult to rise from her chair these days and only did so when necessity required it. John choked back the tears. He found it difficult to speak. She rested her hand patiently on the shoulder of her faithful nephew and waited for the agony she knew was pending.
"Peter," he sobbed. "My life-long friend, Peter."

There was a long pause before he could continue.
"And Paul ……. both dead."
They were gone, both of them on the same day. Paul was beheaded at the side of the road outside the city walls of Rome, whilst Peter was crucified before Nero himself in his garden in the Vallis Vaticana. His persecutor gloated over the fact that Peter requested to be hung in an inverted position because he felt unworthy to die in the same manner as his Lord.
"Of course he may! Let the fool be hung naked with his feet skyward. Let him die slowly. Let us see if the Messiah will come and save him."

Mary and John held each other for a long time, sharing their grief, finding comfort in each other's arms. He sat by her chair and held her hand until she fell asleep, and then he lay at her feet and slept fitfully until another morning came to wake him.

CHAPTER THIRTY ONE

Following the death of Salome, her friend Mary Magdalene entered a period of loneliness which she had not experienced since she was a young woman, before she met Jesus. She had lived an exemplary life of service for the Lord she loved, supporting and often travelling with the apostles as she did when Jesus was in active ministry. She was a woman of substantial means and gave generously to the missionary work. She was a brave and courageous individual and outspoken by nature, preaching the Gospel wherever she went, often rushing in where angels feared to tread. In 69 AD, when rumours were abounding everywhere that Rome was preparing to move with violence against Jerusalem she planned to leave Italy where she had worked for several years in the cause of Christ, but was unsure of exactly where she should go. She had for some time felt a yearning to see her dear friend, Mary, at Ephesus, but never felt that the time was right. She was very much aware that the mother of her Lord was now a very old lady and she wondered if this was the time to make the visit. She had a feeling that there was perhaps some purpose waiting there for her to fulfil. So as the Roman armies closed in around Jerusalem she made the decision that when she felt in prayer that the moment was right she would take ship for Ephesus.

In the April of 70 AD Titus Flavius Vespasian began his assault on Jerusalem. With Tiberius Julius Alexander appointed as his second-in-command he surrounded the city with three legions, the 5th, 12th, and 15th on the western side, and another, the 12th, on the Mount of Olives to the east. So began one of the most terrible sieges of human history with human suffering beyond description and displays of cruelty beyond comprehension. The Jewish historian Josephus claims that more 1,100,000 people were killed during the siege, and another 97,000 captured and enslaved. The sacking of Jerusalem, as prophesied by Jesus, "left not one stone upon another." The beloved city was razed to the ground and its surviving populace scattered across the world. The accuracy of the prophetic words and detailed description of this historic event given by Jesus of Nazareth have been cited as indisputable proof of the validity of Christianity. They certainly add pathos and explanation to the tears which Jesus shed over the city which He loved.

The news of the dark clouds of destruction which had descended upon her beloved Israel was a cloak of extreme heaviness to the mother of the Messiah. She cared deeply about her land and her people. As one born in the lineage of the great King David she was proud of her heritage and a passionate supporter of her kin. She had, however, never forgotten the words which the priest shouted out when the rabble bayed for the blood of her son in the dark early morning of the day of His crucifixion. "His blood be upon us and upon our children" was his cry, and it was taken up and echoed by the religious leaders of the day who were present at the judgment of Jesus. Neither had she forgotten her son's dreadful prophecy of the destruction of Jerusalem. When she heard the news of the gathering storm back in Israel she instinctively knew that the time had come. There was now no way back for her homeland and its capital. The city which was called the City of Peace was being bathed in violence and blood and was destined for centuries to come to be trodden underfoot of the Gentiles. It tore at her heart and tears spilled from her eyes as they had done from those of Jesus thirty-seven years before. She felt so old, so weary with this world of violence and godlessness. Her eighty-six year old body was worn and full of pain. John was very busy working with Timothy, the young pastor of the church in the city, and, apart from occasional visits from some faithful Christians who brought her provisions, she lived a very lonely life. She found it very difficult to move around and she had little to do but pray. She also went through periods of doubt. Her memory was misted with time and the past sometimes feigned unreality. She found herself wondering if there could possibly be a logical explanation for it all. Everything was so long ago and, although Christianity had spread its influence throughout Asia and further afield, it seemed such a long time since she personally saw a miracle and the brutal persecution of the Church continued unabated. Sometimes in her dreams she felt the grotesque presence of the dragon. She thought that the vision of the hideous creature she saw at Calvary when it was sucked into the clouds was the end of it, but she knew that the aura of its evil forever lurked, like a wild beast waiting to pounce. She was basically tired. The evening of her life was well advanced and she was ready for sleep. She whispered, "Please God, take me from this place of pain and into your eternal presence."

Timothy came to see her one day when she was at low ebb. He said he felt directed whilst at prayer to come and read to her a part of a letter which he received from Paul not

long before his execution. He sat at her feet and read her the following words from the great apostle who at the time of writing knew he was approaching the end of his life. He read slowly and deliberately.
"I am now ready to be offered, and the time of my departure is at hand. I have fought a good fight, I have finished my course, I have kept the faith: Henceforth there is laid up for me a crown of righteousness, which the Lord, the righteous Judge, shall give me at that day."

Mary was weeping when he finished. The words were few, but they meant so much to her.
"Thank you, Timothy," she smiled through her tears. "I needed so much to hear that. I have allowed myself to sink in my spirit and the Lord has sent his word to me. If Paul could be so full of optimism in the condemned cell of his prison then how much more can I in my beautiful mountain home! I will stir myself and look forward to my translation as he did to his. I remember how he wrote to the church here that we must 'put on the whole armour of God' because 'we wrestle not against flesh and blood but against principalities and powers.' I will give my spiritual enemies no cause to rejoice over me. Sing with me, Timothy! Let the hills hear the sound of my rejoicing!"

They sang a psalm together. Her voice was feeble and his was quite tuneless and it sounded worse than dreadful, but the presence of the Holy Spirit filled the room. She knew from times past that He always comes to those who sing His praise. They then broke bread together in remembrance of the body and blood of the Lord, giving thanks for His immense sacrifice for the souls of

humankind. Her eyes were shining like those of a young woman in love as Timothy took his leave. She struggled to her feet and made it to the door, leaning heavily against the doorpost. Timothy reached the footpath which would lead him down the hill to the city, but before the trees swallowed him from her sight he turned and lifted his hand in an affectionate farewell.
"See you, Mary," he called.
She weakly lifted her hand in response.
"See you, Timothy," she whispered. "But I think not in this world."

As the weeks passed by and spring gave way to summer months the pain in her stomach drastically worsened. Her appetite for food was now gone and her flesh was dropping from her fragile bones. Her white hair was thin and wispy and she could feel her cheekbones protruding above her sunken cheeks. Her skin was dry and wizened with age. She now thought much about home, about Joseph's children and the grandchildren she had never seen.
She also meditated about times long ago, about her childhood and about the occasions after Salome was married, when they sat together by the lake and watched the fishing boats trimming their sails to the wind. Most of all she longed for her favourite hill in Nazareth, the fresh air of her homeland, the scent of the wild flowers and the feeling of the wind in her hair as in her youth she ran down the grassy slopes to sit gasping on the well in the valley below.

She had heard it said that people know when they are going to die. She never really believed it until the day the knowledge of it came to her. She just woke up one morning with recognition in her spirit that this was her final day on earth. She just knew. She also knew that if she was going to die she wanted it to be outside in the warm summer air and not in the dark interior of her home, but she had no one to carry her outside. News had reached John that his life-long friend, Andrew, brother of Simon Peter, had been executed by crucifixion in Greece and he was down in the town talking with Timothy and the elders of the church. It was a sad time for John. Soon he would be the only one left of those who walked physically with Jesus.

Mary was if nothing else a very determined lady. If she wanted to be outside she would somehow find a way to get there, or die in the attempt. She picked up the walking stick that one of the men from the church had cut for her from the branch of a tree and hauled herself to her feet. Holding tightly to the stick with one hand and dragging a woollen blanket behind her with the other she step by step shuffled towards the open door. She stood for a while leaning against the wall before stepping outside into the sunshine of a perfect summer's day. The mountain air felt so good as she breathed it hungrily into her lungs. She stumbled a few yards more towards the place that would give her clear view of the peaceful sea beyond the valley and then succumbed to her weakness. She sank slowly to the grassy sod beneath the branches of an old pine tree. It took several more minutes for her to arrange her blanket before painfully easing herself onto it. She sat and looked out towards the west. The sun was climbing above the forest behind her and soothing her aching back with its

warm rays. She was ready. She who had conceived alone would die alone.
"Oh God of Abraham!" she whispered. "Please take away my pain."

Someone once told her that when it is time to die Jesus comes for you. That would be wonderful, she had not seen Him for so long, but she didn't believe that either. How could He possible come in person for every dying Christian, unless He somehow did it through the person of the omnipresent Holy Spirit?

By midday she was hot and very thirsty and she realised that she had no water to drink. Her energy was now zero and there was no way that she could even crawl back into the house. The pain was unbearable and she lapsed into a state of delirium. Her mind was revisiting a scene from long ago and she was once more gazing on the bruised and bleeding form of her son as He hung in the darkness of Golgotha. He was struggling to speak. She could just make out his words as He forced them through his swollen lips.
"I thirst, I thirst, I thirst."
She came to her senses muttering, "I thirst, I thirst, I thirst."
By 3p.m. her breathing was shallow, but the pain seemed to have eased. She tried to look out across the valley, but it seemed as though a premature darkness had settled over the entire landscape. She closed her weary eyes and lay back exhausted. She could feel the heat of the sun piercing the foliage above her head, but she could see nothing.

"It's so dark," she whispered through her cracked parched lips. "It is so very dark."
She wanted Joseph, wanted him to hold her hand and kiss her with his cool lips. She missed him so much. She wondered if he would recognise her now, so changed from the bright young thing he loved so much.

She suffered on until the day began to die, the sun sliding inexorably towards the western horizon, casting its evening glow over the motionless form of the dying saint. How insignificant she looked as her shrunken body adopted the curled up form of a babe within its mother's womb. Suddenly she thought that she could see again. She could see the sun being gently lowered into the sea. Then she saw it and her soul sank with horror. It was the dragon, alive, powerful, angry, its pernicious face framed in the blood of the setting sun, rising enormous from the valley. Its huge bloodshot eyes were hungry for vengeance, its filthy jaws stretched to devour, its tongue lusting to destroy the fragile enemy which lay powerless in its path.

"I thought that you were dead."
She only mouthed the words, no sound was forthcoming, but inside she was screaming them.
Thunder roared from the throat of the beast as it supplanted the edge of the cliff and slid on its belly towards its helpless victim. It seemed as though the smell of hell rose like smoke from its scaly form. She tried to call the name of Jesus, but no words would come. A great weight was pressing down on her chest, preventing the cry. She struggled in the throes of death and mouthed the name which is above all other names. She didn't really say it. It

was not spoken. It was more like a thought which with superhuman effort she pushed through a barrier in her brain. The result was more powerful than anything she had ever seen or known. She saw a man's hand, as big as the mountain. It swung with the speed of lightening and the back of it connected with the dragon's head and sent it sprawling across the heavens. She heard the scream of anguish which accompanied its journey as it became smaller and smaller, until it disappeared into the void of nowhere. Above the scream of her enemy she heard a voice like the sound of many waters, deep, powerful, like a two-edged sword issuing from the mouth of divinity. The words were words which she heard almost four decades before from the dying lips of her son.

"It is finished!"

The huge hand withdrew from her vision and as it did so she saw the scar where the nail pierced it. It was the hand of her Son.

All was silent now, like the aftermath of a storm. Her pain was gone. A soft breeze blew in from the sea and the evening was cool. Mary was still, at perfect peace. Her breathing was shallow and intermittent. She thought that she could hear music in the distance, the like of which she had never heard before. It was soft and consoling to her spirit and there was the sound of singing, the harmonies of angelic voices mingling with those of the redeemed. Then the most beautiful light she had ever seen mantled the grassy slope. It was not brilliant or blinding, but reminiscent of a crystal pool, calm and inviting, and in its centre the figure of a man. He was so beautiful, so pure, so strong and holy. She wanted to go to Him, but as she tried to rise He stepped forward and took her hand as though to lift her to her feet.

"Come mother," He said. "It's time to go home."

The sun was not yet fully set and the paling light was still strong enough to show her the way as Mary Magdalene stepped from the path between the trees and walked slowly towards the house of her old friend. Gone was the burning red hair of her youth and her once erect back was now somewhat bent with her seventy-two years. Her face was ruddy from the long walk, but her features still showed evidence of the beauty with which she was once endowed. It had not taken her long to find John when she arrived in Ephesus and he gladly gave her the directions to Mary's home. It took her more than an hour to make the climb from the city, but her heart was elated with the anticipation of her expected reunion. She tapped gently on the door which readily swung open at her touch revealing an empty room.

"Mary," she called. "Are you there?"

She stepped inside and called again, but no reply. Feeling a little anxious and perplexed she walked outside and instantly saw what she took to be the sleeping form of her old friend. She approached carefully for fear of startling her and lowered herself into a sitting position at her side. She immediately saw that she was dead. She touched the flesh of her face, still warm, then bent and tenderly kissed her forehead. With tears trickling down her face she cradled Mary's head in her lap and stroked the top of her head. Her mind went back to a day long ago when the roles were reversed, her head on Mary's knees, waking to see the kind eyes of a stranger smiling gently into her own and hearing her ask her name. They stood facing each other that day, four hands clasped in a friendship which was set to span a lifetime. The difference was that Mary was not going to open her eyes. Her earthly journey was complete and she would never know that the Lord who saw this day from the beginning had sent the younger to tend and bury the elder.

EPILOGUE

Mary Magdalene stayed in Ephesus to help the Apostle John until she died. Legend has it that relics from her body were later transported to France.

The Apostle John lived in Ephesus for the rest of his life. After Mary's death he wrote his Gospel and the three letters which are found in the New Testament. In 94 AD, when he was an old man of eighty-one, Emperor Domitian decreed that he be exiled to the island called Patmos where he received the amazing Revelation of Jesus Christ which is now the last book in the Bible. He was released after the death of Domitian and moved back to Ephesus in 96 AD. Four years later at the age of eighty-seven he was defending an assault against the reputation of Mary the mother of Jesus when he was arrested and, contrary to general opinion, was executed by decapitation in fulfilment of the words of Jesus, "Ye shall indeed drink of the cup that I drink of; and with the baptism that I am baptised withal shall ye be baptised." He was the last of the twelve apostles to die. His tomb can be visited today in the excavated site of ancient Ephesus in Turkey.

The church in Ephesus became the major centre for the spreading of the Christian message throughout Asia Minor and beyond. The Temple of Diana was destroyed in 262 AD by an invasion of the Goths who laid it waste and set fire to it. Because most Ephesians were turning to Christianity it was never rebuilt. The site of the Temple was rediscovered in 1869 by an expedition sponsored by the British Museum. Today a single column of the Temple can be seen on the site, a stark reminder of the lost glory of Diana.

Mary went home to a world where afflictions and suffering do not exist, where pain and tears are known no more, to a world where sorrow holds no sway, and sin and shame are wiped away. To a world where beauty is unsullied by passing time and all is as God intended it to be. In this blessed place of peace she sits and bows before her Lord and King, and yet, as she looks upon his nail-scarred hands, the hands which she held when He was just a boy, she cannot help remembering that He, the exalted Son of God, is still flesh of her flesh and bone of her bones.

Mary's sister Salome, accompanied by her sons, James and John, once asked Jesus if her two sons could sit on each side of Him in his kingdom. He replied that the honour was not His to give but his Father's. He indicated that in this spiritual realm there has to be a cross before a crown and suffering before glory and only those willing to be baptised with the baptism of suffering, which He so willingly embraced, could qualify for such a privilege. Many thousands of people have suffered in the cause of Christ across the centuries, often paying the ultimate price of martyrdom, so only God knows to whom such honour will be given. We can, however, be forgiven for some speculation, or even for the hazarding of a calculated guess. I just wonder, when all this is over and His bride, the Church, assembles for the feast of feasts, and seats are assigned for the marriage supper of the Lamb, I wonder who will humbly take the angel's arm and be led to that very special seat of honour at the right hand of the Saviour? It doesn't have to be a man does it?

About the Author

John Hibbert was born in Wakefield, Yorkshire, in 1946. From the earliest age he had an unusual desire to know God and throughout his teenage years spent his weekends travelling about the country to listen to the most well-known preachers in the U.K. In 1967 he left a promising career in engineering to become a preacher of the Gospel himself, serving for five years in Rotherham before moving to Mansfield Woodhouse, where he has worked tirelessly with his fellow ministers to build the Church of Jesus Christ, to the present day. He has never wavered from his adherence to the tenets of Holy Scripture as the only true standard for Christian living. Regarded by some as a controversial figure, he has fearlessly stood against the increasing trend to compromise truth at the demands of a liberal society.

He has three happily-married daughters, one son and six grandchildren. He has lived through the joy and pain of fatherhood, shown a remarkable and consistent commitment to caring for people and considers himself to be only at the beginning of the fulfilment of his true calling, which is world evangelism.

He has a wide experience of life, both its pleasures and its sufferings, has extensively travelled around the world in the cause of Christ and has developed a deeply-felt empathy with the feelings of people past and present. He delights to look beyond the obvious, explore the reasons and origins behind the facts, and tell the story as he believes it was, without condemnation or misplaced adoration.

Printed in the United Kingdom by
Lightning Source UK Ltd., Milton Keynes
139172UK00001B/2/P